SOM

The Royal Diaries

Catherine

The Great Journey

BY KRISTIANA GREGORY

Scholastic Inc. New York

Prussia
1743

7 August 1743
Zerbst, Prussia

The view of the river from this castle makes me thirsty. It has been a hot summer. The window here in our library is open for a breeze, and I've been leaning out over the sill, thankful for the cool air and thankful my lessons are over for the day.

Tutors come for every academic subject: mathematics, literature, science; also for dance and music. My favorite is Mademoiselle Babette. She instructs me daily in manners and her French language, though I speak with a slight German accent. It was she who gave me this journal for my birthday last April.

It fits nicely in my lap when I'm sitting, and I keep it hidden in a hatbox under some feathers arranged just so. This way I'll know if someone tries to look inside. Also in the box is a jug of ink with a stopper and a knife to sharpen my quills.

"A girl of fourteen is ready to describe the world around her," Mademoiselle told me after I had unwrapped her gift.

Why I've avoided doing so these past four months, I don't know. Perhaps it's shyness, the way I sometimes feel when making new friends or learning something new. It takes me a while to get used to the idea.

So here I am, dear diary, at long last, ready to tell you my secrets. . . .

Next Day

Finally, it has stopped raining and we are waiting in the courtyard for Friedrich's birthday party to begin. He is nine years old today and very proud of his new soldier's uniform. Presently, he is marching back and forth between the palace walls. His black boots are already wet from stomping in the puddles, for he likes to scare the ducks. I am glad the sword Papá gave him is wooden because the way my brother is waving it around, he could hurt someone.

Some of the children from the village are arriving through the castle gate with their small, wrapped gifts. The boys have on their black caps and vests, the girls are wearing clean white aprons over their dresses. Their voices are high with excitement. In a moment I will join them.

I am sitting in the shade, under an open window of the grand salon. I can hear Mother upstairs. She is angry again, and I can tell she is looking out at the children and the hot sun.

". . . befitting a German prince . . . It is not fair. . . ." These are words she often says when complaining about our poverty, though she herself is a princess from a small royal family. At my birthday in April, villagers brought baskets of soft pretzels and *Pfeffernuesse,* my favorite little cookies rolled in powdered sugar. I was touched, truly.

But Mother believes our guests should be dukes and counts bearing elegant gifts, such as jewels and invitations to visit their castles. She does not understand that many of these nobles ignore her because her temper explodes at the slightest thing. It's not fun being with someone who is always mad. At least this is what our maids tell me.

Oh, the children are lining up for games. . . . The party has begun!

After Friedrich's Party . . .

Because the day was hot, my brother suggested that all the children — there were nearly thirty of us — remove our clothes and jump into the stream! There was a terrible silence as Mother drew in a deep breath. Before she could explode, Papá led us out through the gate and down to a narrow sandy beach, then handed each one of us a stick with some string. We were to make our own boats and float them on the tiny waves lapping the shore.

Well! You would have thought Papá had made us drink poison. Mother's face turned red. The curled wig on her head jiggled as she waved her arms.

"For God's sake," she said. "Friedrich is a *prince*, not a commoner." Then she lifted the hem of her dress and headed back to the palace. I could hear the *click-click-click* of her shoes as she hurried along the stone path. The wide hoop under her skirt bobbed up and down with every step.

Midnight

Am now in my nightgown. The tall windows in my room are open to the night. It is still warm out. The rooftops are dark save for an attic window here and there flickering with candlelight. Beyond the palace, there are torches along the riverbank. I can smell a charcoal fire where fishermen must be cooking a late supper.

Mademoiselle Babette is plump and cheerful, always

chattering in French. When she came in to say good night, she brought a message from Mother. I'm to meet her tomorrow in the garden for another Discussion.

That is why I haven't been able to fall asleep. These talks always end with one of us in tears.

The Discussion

Mademoiselle woke me this morning by opening the shutters. Bright sunlight filled the room. After I splashed water on my face from the basin, she brushed and braided my hair. It is almost to my waist and is the color of my amber necklace, a golden brown. My blue vest laced in front with ribbons looked nice over my dress. The sleeves of my blouse buttoned from my wrist to my elbow. I felt elegant. But when I entered the garden, Mother shook her head.

"My poor German princess," she said. "You're as plain as a toad. Who will ever want to marry you?"

I sat on a bench by the fountain. Songbirds flitted down for a drink, then flew off when I dipped my hand in the water. The problem is this:

Unless I marry someone in line to be a king, I am doomed — my whole family is doomed — to this lowly station in life. Papá is merely a major general in the

Prussian army with no royal blood. In Mother's opinion he never amounted to anything except to be a boring Lutheran.

"You know, dear," she said, leaning close enough that I could smell cheese on her breath, "I was just fifteen when your papá and I wed. He was old enough to be a grandfather. You can't imagine how my mother wept. She had wanted me to marry a king, not a soldier, but it was the best arrangement my family could make. We were neither rich nor popular."

At this I looked into my mother's eyes. They are blue, like mine. A crease in her forehead makes her look worried, but when she smiles I think she is pretty.

I wish she would smile more often.

Mother stood to walk around the fountain and back again. She listed a few dukes and counts who might be looking for a bride. How she sighed when describing King Louis XV of France — if only he had a nephew or son who wanted me, then I (and she) could live at Versailles, the grandest palace in Europe.

The most likely marriage for me would be with Charles-Peter Ulrich of Holstein, a German duke. He and I met when I was ten. . . . I am not fond of the memory, but Mother insists on retelling every detail.

My quill has scraped the ink jug dry. . . .

Later

I am thankful ink powder is not expensive, for I would be lonely without you, dear diary.

To continue about Charles-Peter . . . Mother loves the excitement of travel and that it takes her away from her dull life here in Zerbst. Being around nobility fills her with smiles and sizzling gossip. So when we received an invitation to a royal party four summers ago, she was thrilled.

We were at our palace in Stettin — the village where I was born — which is far north from here on the Oder River. Our ship left from the dock and followed the river to the Baltic Sea.

I stood on deck with Mademoiselle. The wind hit my face as if I were riding a fast horse. It was thrilling to breathe salt air and feel the waves roll under our hull. For hours we followed the northern coast among islands and inlets to the port city of Kiel.

We stayed in a castle on a rocky bluff. The occasion was a wedding attended by royals from all over Europe. I remember their tall, powdered wigs, and a stench, for many of them apparently were not in the habit of bathing. Some of the ladies wore small satin sacks around their necks as if they were pieces of jewelry. These bags contained spices and rose petals, but were not much help to clear the air.

One afternoon at this party, Mother introduced me to a boy about my age, nudging me to curtsy. "Figchen, he is your second cousin," — this is where Mother leaned down to whisper in my ear — "*and* grandson of Peter the Great. He's in line to be king of Sweden."

I will stop here to mention that Figchen is the most pleasant of my many nicknames. It means "darling Sophie." My full title is Sophie Augusta Fredericka, Princess of Anhalt-Zerbst. It is short compared to other royal girls. I like hearing it much better than "ugly" or "duck-face."

* * *

Mother thinks it is high and mighty to be related to Peter the Great. He was the Russian czar who stood nearly seven feet tall. I have heard stories about him my whole life. My favorite is about the dwarfs. He once had a party with a parade through his palace — seventy-two dwarfs dressed in Russian costume marched by twos into the grand salon. I cannot imagine such a sight!

Then a giant pie the size of a coach was rolled out to the center of the room. Someone lowered a silver sword into the crust to break it open, and out jumped two dwarfs — singing! What no one has explained to me is how that crust was baked without cooking the little people.

"Czar" is what Russians call their emperor; "czarina" is their empress. One morning when Papá and I were walking in the courtyard, he explained the title. He said the word comes from Latin, describing the most famous emperor of all time, Caesar.

Back to the Royal Grandson . . .

I always feel bad when Mother reminds me that I am neither pretty nor rich, and I wish she would stop mentioning my cousin Charles-Peter. Truly, at first sight I thought he was a girl. His face was soft and pale, his hair curled to his shoulders.

The castle in Kiel where we stayed had a children's playroom with windows looking out to sea. Charles-Peter showed me rows of tin soldiers standing on the sills. They had brightly painted jackets of red, white pants, and black knee-high boots. He told me they were watching for enemy ships.

"They are only stupid dolls," I said. Again, I was just ten years old at the time. This remark so upset him, he took a wooden sword and knocked the soldiers out the window, one by one. He made exploding sounds with his mouth as if they'd been shot.

"There," he said, "see what you've done, you nasty little

girl?" He stomped over to a small table where there were carafes of wine and other drinks. He poured himself a glass of an amber liquid that he downed in one gulp.

I was repulsed because there was a foul odor about his person. When I told him he stank, he said, "I have never had a bath in my life, I never will, and no one can make me."

This is the boy Mother wants me to marry.

17 August 1743, Zerbst

My sister, Elizabeth, is eight months old today. Ulrike — my name for her — is the darling of our castle because she sings! Not any melodies we can recognize, but her voice rises and falls with a sweetness that reminds me of a robin. She crawls everywhere, which means dirty knees and a scolding from Mother if she notices. The ladies work themselves to tears trying to keep our little princess tidy.

Her wet nurse was dismissed yesterday. Ulrike cried long into the night because she is used to a nipple to help her sleep. I will try to distract her with a story this evening. Maybe I will tell her about our cousin's toy soldiers that flew out the window.

Dear diary, I am so happy to have you. . . . Everyone is mad at me today! By myself, I waded in the stream to cool off. The day was too hot for Mademoiselle's assignments — fourteen pages of Molière to be translated from French into German, what torture! I slipped out the gate when the guard turned away. He did not see me because he was blowing his nose against the wall.

It was wonderful to be alone, without tutors or ladies-in-waiting. Soon enough, some children from the village saw me and came alongside so we could skip rocks into the water. We even went in up to our waists, letting our skirts float up at our sides.

But when I returned late in the afternoon, Mother was in a fury. She boxed my ears and slapped me until I felt blood in my mouth. It hurt, but I refused to let her see me cry.

"A common girl," she yelled. "That's all you are. You'll be lucky to become a fishwife, if that. Is this what you want, to disgrace your family?"

I ran to my suite, passing Mademoiselle Babette in the hall. She said nothing, but stared straight ahead. A red welt on her cheek made me wonder if Mother had struck her, too. When my door was latched behind me, I tapped on my wall to see if Friedrich was in his room. We have a secret knock when we're lonely and want each other's company, but this time there was no response. I threw myself onto my bed and wept.

A mirror hangs above my writing desk. I am tormented by my reflection! Why can't I be beautiful? My nose is long and narrow, my chin sticks out, and I have pimples. There is nothing lovely about me! At least my teeth aren't black with rot like some people I know whose names I won't mention here.

Three Days Later

Mademoiselle Babette and I discuss many subjects and share many secrets. She tells me I'm smart and capable of great things, that it is good I love her native language and can speak it fluently.

"Figchen, no person of quality can afford to be ignorant of French," she says, always holding her finger in the air for emphasis. She has challenged me to record everything in my diary *en français*, to keep my pen fluent as well. There is another good reason:

Mother can only read German and a little Swedish.

The Portrait

It is three o'clock in the morning, and I am sitting on my bedroom floor by the window. The shutters are open to reveal a moonlit village. It appears that all are sleeping. My candle is tall, so I can write until sunrise if I want to.

Moments ago I bolted awake. Something that Mother said during our Discussion the other day haunts me. Last December, just days after she gave birth to baby Ulrike in Berlin, she took me by carriage to a tall stone building on the other side of town.

The purpose of our visit? To meet the French painter Antoine Pesne.

In his *atelier*, his studio, he positioned me by a window that reached to the ceiling. The drapes had been removed to let in as much of the gray winter light as possible. I stood there for hours, turned slightly toward him, my hands poised at my waist. I was not allowed to speak, for even my mouth had to remain still. His French was like Babette's, easy to understand. He explained that he had been hired by Elizabeth Petrovna, Empress of Russia, to paint my portrait.

She wants to see what I look like.

As this artist studied my hair and cheeks and neck,

dabbing colors onto canvas, he revealed a small secret: Portraits of young noble ladies from all over Europe are being sent to St. Petersburg, to meet with the empress's approval. Or not.

She wants to find a bride for her nephew, Charles-Peter. It seems my cousin will not be king of Sweden after all. He now lives in Russia under the empress's watchful eye because she has declared him heir to *her* throne. When she dies, he will become czar of the entire Russian Empire. His bride will be empress.

My cousin's new title is Grand Duke Peter. He is being forced to abandon his Lutheran upbringing, which is like mine, and embrace the Orthodox religion. I wonder if the empress will also insist that he bathe.

* * *

I watched Monsieur Pesne's face as he worked. A blue smock tied with a sash fell to his knees. He wore no wig, but instead a beret that covered his left ear. His black eyebrows looked like caterpillars.

Please make me pretty, I wanted to say. *Please don't show my pimples.* But I kept silent. I dared not breathe what was in my heart. Fear. Embarrassment. Mother has made it clear that I am unattractive. But at that moment I decided I would just stand tall.

If Her Imperial Majesty, the empress, will see no beauty in Figchen, perhaps she will instead see my character. As for my cousin, he has no say in the matter of his marriage.

So, dear diary, all these months later, why am I awake at four o'clock in the morning?

Alas, two gentlemen from the Russian court arrived yesterday to get a close look at me and ask questions. They are taking their report back to St. Petersburg, along with *another* portrait of me, to be painted this week.

I am distressed to be stared at and spoken about as if I were an antique chair.

During afternoon tea, Mother was so happy with these gentlemen sitting in her salon that she rose to her best behavior. She spoke sweetly to me while offering a plate of *Pfeffernuesse,* as if we were bosom friends.

The Russians spoke to us in German. I liked their accents, but I did not like how Mother tried to drop French phrases into the conversation. When one of them mentioned that a rainstorm had flooded the road, she meant to say *C'est dommage,* "That's a pity." But what she really said was *C'est frommage,* meaning "That's cheese."

One of the men choked a bit on his cookie before recovering his good manners. He nodded at Mother with a smile.

Later in the afternoon, Mother found me in my parlor playing with Ulrike. As gently as possible, I mentioned her error. She narrowed her eyes at me, then picked up a vase from the bookshelf. It was crystal, a gift to me from Babette, now full of beautiful summer roses.

"My, aren't you a smart one?" she said, walking to the open window. She leaned out and let go of the vase. It was a few seconds before I heard it shatter in the courtyard below.

My heart felt so chilled, I could not speak. Instead, I pulled my sister into my lap and held her close.

A Hot Afternoon

It took two weeks for the new artist to create my likeness. When I wasn't posing in painful silence, the visiting Russians engaged me in every type of conversation. They often switched from German to French to test my fluency in what they say is the court's language of diplomacy.

Mother was always in the room, smiling and nodding to me as if her eyes could speak correct answers. She pretended to understand, but I knew our rapid French slipped by her.

Those two gentlemen rode from our courtyard early this morning, just as the sun was rising over a bend in the river. I watched from an upstairs window as their horses and baggage carts clattered along the cobbled streets on their way out of the city, back to Russia.

One of those carts carried the new portrait of me. The oils had yet to dry, so the canvas had been packed between open crates that did not touch its moist surface. It occurred to me that insects or other bugs could land in the wet paint and distort my image. What if, at long last, the empress was able to see this painting only to find a wasp stuck to my forehead?

While I worried over this possibility, I sat on the floor hugging my knees, the marble cool to my bare feet. Birds in the courtyard were flying up to their nests in the eaves.

A shout startled me.

"Poor posture!" cried my mother. "Up with you, girl, or we'll bring in the hangman again. No one wants a poor German princess with a crooked back." Mother took such a deep breath to continue her rage, I thought her corset would pop open.

Her words filled me with a sick dread.

Now it is late afternoon. I am writing from a narrow table pushed against the window, where I can feel a breeze. The aroma of roasted meat and onions is making me hungry. A young servant girl just leaned into the room and announced — in French — that dinner is served. She must be newly arrived from France because I have not seen her before. Shall continue this later.

After Supper

Friedrich and I sat across from each other at the table, our parents on opposite ends. Dinner was a tureen of spinach soup with buttered black bread. Our baby sister was in the kitchen with her maid, who feeds her with a spoon. Ulrike is messy. If food isn't to her liking she spits it out, then smears it with her fingers on anything she can reach. She causes such an uproar, Mother will not allow her into the dining hall.

I ate quickly so I could get back to you, dear diary. All the windows are open in my room, and the night breeze is warm. From the village square I can hear an accordion and gay laughter. There must be a dance. Though the sun has set, the sky is still light enough that I do not need a candle.

To continue . . . At the age of seven, I suffered from pneumonia while living at our castle in Stettin. When at last I began to feel better, the ladies in attendance bathed me with hot sponges. As they began dressing me, they noticed my back had become crooked from so many weeks in bed, coughing and so forth. My left shoulder was much lower than the right, and looking at myself in the mirror I saw that I resembled the letter Z.

I did not think it so terrible, but my parents were

horrified. Their homely daughter was now also a cripple. They whispered and conferred and swore the ladies to secrecy.

How will Figchen ever wear a crown of jewels if she cannot stand up straight? I heard them say. *A royal bride must have correct posture.*

On and on they worried.

Finally, one morning a villager was brought into my suite. He held his hat in his hands, glancing around the room. The hat was black, as were his coat and trousers. His shoes were caked with mud, but for once Mother did not seem bothered by such a shabby visitor.

I did not know who he was or why he was allowed to look at me.

About the Hangman

After some moments, Mother led me behind a screen and unbuttoned my dress, leaving me in a cotton shift that fell to my knees. To my humiliation, she pushed me out into the room near a window, to stand in a pool of sunlight.

The man examined me, even pressing his rough hands against the bare skin of my back. I wanted to die from embarrassment, but Mother's steely look told me to be

21

silent. Later, I was to learn that it was his knowledge of ropes and pulleys that afforded him this honorable, but secret, job.

The next day he returned with a frame for my torso. It seemed to be nothing more than an elaborate corset, but I could hardly breathe as he laced me into it. He then wrapped a thick black ribbon across my right shoulder, then around my right arm, tying it securely behind me. I felt stiff as a scarecrow. From that day forward, only the trusted maids were allowed to dress me and help me maneuver over the chamber pot. How I hated this! The nights were long, and sleep often didn't come until the wee hours of morning because I had so much trouble getting comfortable.

Day and night, month after month I wore this equipment, only removing everything to change my underclothes. The hangman visited every other morning to see how I was doing and make adjustments, mainly to tighten and cinch. I wondered if this is what he did at the scaffolds in Stettin, and with such a grim thought in my mind I could not look him in the eye.

After nearly two years, he noticed my spine had begun to straighten. Just before we sailed to Kiel, my corset was at long last thrown into the fire. Of course my parents were overjoyed. Finally, I was presentable enough to meet Charles-Peter and the other royals.

This is why Mother mentioning the hangman this afternoon made me feel so dreadful.

27 August 1743, Zerbst

One year ago today, my favorite brother, Wilhelm, died of a fever. He was eleven, I was thirteen. Mother crumbled to the floor when the doctors whispered the terrible news to her. I remember that she was large with child and how she lay in the hallway clinging to her maid, inconsolable. Grief still clings to Mother like a dark cloak. At the mention of my brother's name, her eyes water and she turns away.

A few months later my sister, Elizabeth — Ulrike — was born in Berlin. Mother named her after the Russian ruler, and in early spring, couriers came by sleigh from Russia with a gift. It was a portrait of Empress Elizabeth framed in diamonds — she is Ulrike's godmother!

I do not know how my mother arranged this relationship, but she was thrilled.

"Finally," she said, "we're linked to *real* royalty." Apparently, the gift also signaled to Mother that the empress had more than a casual interest in our family.

But why me? I wonder. If I am so ugly and so poor, why is the empress even considering me for her nephew's bride?

During a history lesson, Mademoiselle Babette explained about royal weddings. "They are nothing more than politics, *ma chèrie.* A chess game with real kings, real queens, and real pawns."

I cringed inside to think it was all just a game. "Is it so?" I asked Mademoiselle. "That I am a pawn?"

"Facts are facts." She shrugged, her palms turned upward in that charming French gesture. "The Empress of Russia has no husband and is getting on in years. She's desperate to continue her family line, and since that pitiful little Charles-Peter is her only heir, she must find him a bride. That way there'll be children, and someone to inherit the throne."

When she saw the look of disappointment on my face she said, "I know, *chèrie,* I know. It's not one bit romantic, but even the French do these sorts of things."

Before Bed

Mademoiselle Babette just came in and handed me a short candle, one inch tall. This way I won't stay up late tonight writing.

Mother's orders are that I must sleep more. "The

empress does not want a feeble girl with dark circles under the eyes," she said. "Charles-Peter's bride must be perfectly healthy."

This new rule reminds me of when Mother took away all my dolls and toys. I was seven years old. She said I no longer needed such frivolities (she called them) because I was now a big girl.

Truth be told, dolls hadn't been much fun because their porcelain heads break if you drop them, and their tiny black shoes are always falling off. It's odd knowing she wants me to marry a boy who does little else than play with tin soldiers and make rude sounds with his mouth.

I have a confession. Though Charles-Peter is a wretched boy, I believe I could bear being his wife, so sweet does the title of "empress" sound to my ears. Alas, since I am merely a pawn, I shall let myself be moved toward the throne.

When I told this to Mademoiselle Babette, she said I am ambitious for being only fourteen years of age. But I think a better word for this situation is *practical*. Because I must wed, I may as well better my family's name rather than disgrace it by marrying someone with no future.

Candle is out.

31 December 1743, Zerbst

Four long months have passed without writing!

Dear diary, you've been lost until just moments ago, when Mademoiselle Babette brought in my hatbox just discovered this morning in the attic.

The story of what happened was slow to unravel, but here it is:

One afternoon last summer, as the sun was setting, Friedrich and I went out to the courtyard, to the western wall. Deep shade made it a cool place to play, so we made up a game drawing with chalk on the stones. When we were called in for dinner I returned to my room, only to discover the cupboard door was open. I didn't think much about it until I realized my hatbox was missing — with my diary! I felt short of breath, such was my panic.

Mother ordered a search. Everyone from the kitchen staff to dusting maids was questioned, yet no one admitted to having seen or heard anything suspicious.

Mademoiselle offered a tablet so I could keep writing, but it didn't feel the same. There was no cover or way to tie the pages closed, and besides, I kept thinking any day now my real diary would be found. But weeks passed. Autumn arrived with its falling leaves and cold nights, then the first snowstorm. Christmas came and went.

Now just this afternoon — on the eve of our New Year — that young French serving girl was caught stealing Ulrike's silver spoon. She had slipped it into her apron pocket, then hurried to the attic. What she didn't know was that two servants had witnessed the act and followed her upstairs. As soon as they stepped through the small doorway from the hall, the extent of the maid's crime was discovered. My hatbox was there along with a trove of other treasures: Mother's brooches, earrings, lace collars, assorted silk stockings and handkerchiefs, silverware, and a golden goblet.

Over time, Mother had noticed these items were missing, but didn't know where to look.

This girl was dismissed immediately, of course, but not before suffering a whipping in the great hall, in front of other servants who were ordered to watch. I could hear her cries echo through the corridors, but my heart was cold. At that very moment I was looking through these pages and had seen smudges from dirty fingers.

She had read my diary.

1 January 1744, Zerbst

It is nearly eleven o'clock at night, but I'm unable to sleep. Wind is spitting snow against my windowpanes. A blizzard has been blowing for several hours now. Even though it makes my room colder, I like the shutters to stay open so I can look outside.

Throughout the evening, Papá and Mother secluded themselves in the library. For hours visitors came and went, the tall heavy doors closed tightly so I couldn't eavesdrop. Puddles were tracked in along every corridor. Finally, Mother ordered me to bed, but Mademoiselle Babette was kind enough to give me a tall candle.

So here I am, writing late. What happened is this:

Just after dinner, while we were still at the table waiting for dessert to be served, a courier from Berlin arrived with a packet of letters. His cloak was covered with snow because of the storm.

Papá untied the string and looked through the envelopes. He squinted at the handwriting of one in particular, his eyebrows arched, then he handed it to Mother.

Leaning close, I recognized the penmanship of a Russian grand duke with whom she's been corresponding for a number of years. Written across the top was *Personal! Very Urgent! To the Very High and Well-born Princess Johanna Elizabeth of Anhalt-Zerbst, in her Castle of Zerbst.*

Mother broke open the seal, which was a stamp of purple wax, and thumbed through the parchments — the letter was twelve pages long! — then she began to read silently.

Still leaning close, I saw the words, ". . . *with the princess, her elder daughter . . ."* I drew in a breath. The duke was referring to me!

"Figchen," said Mother, putting the letter facedown on the table, "go to your room immediately."

Wondering . . .

Now it is midnight. The tall oak clock in the hallway is chiming twelve, the *slowest* clangs I have ever heard.

The storm has stopped. I can see outside to the windows across the courtyard downstairs. They are aglow with candles. How late will everyone stay up talking?

I wonder if Empress Elizabeth has sent for Mother and me. Maybe my portrait arrived in good shape after all, and the likeness pleased her. I feel in my heart this is so and that she has decided I'm to be Peter's bride.

Tomorrow I will beg Mother to tell me if this is to be.

2 January 1744, Zerbst

Mother won't talk to me. If it's as I suspect — that the letter *does* concern me — why won't she say anything? Why does she want to keep me in the dark?

I am so frustrated! Doesn't she know I'm miserable when she ignores me?

3 January 1744, Zerbst

Snow. Lots more has covered the courtyard. I spend much time at my desk, studying, but today I'm allowing myself to be distracted by looking out the window. Something outside has amused me . . . for the past hour, there have been three servant boys with shovels. They are supposed to be clearing a path to the road, but instead are throwing snowballs at one another.

Mademoiselle stood with me, watching. She, too, laughed. "French boys, German boys, they are all the same," she said. "One boy is a job done, two boys is half a job done, but three boys is nothing but mischief."

At breakfast while Mother was spreading marmalade on her bread, she managed a smile for me. I mistook her friendliness and asked about the letter.

"Shh!" she said. Then setting down her knife, she slapped my hand.

I wanted to cry from its sting, but instead excused myself from the table with a curtsy.

During grammar lessons, Friedrich brought his book to my room so we could study together. His French is coming along, although he prefers that we speak to each other in German. It's easier for him to express himself in our native tongue, though — for me — French is now as easy as breathing.

"Figchen," he said, "just go to Mother's room and ask for the secret. Don't leave until she tells you, even if it makes her angry."

I opened his book to a page of verbs and handed him a pencil. His young face looked so hopeful, I didn't tell him Mother scares me. It ties my stomach in knots when she's mad.

Later

If I ever become empress, I will make a law that parents cannot strike their daughters, nor torture them with silence. My mother has always been mean. But as I try to understand her, I think her hunger for power has made her more so.

4 January 1744, Zerbst

Early this morning I did a bold thing after all, and knocked on Mother's door. When her voice called "*Entrez*," I stepped inside.

"Please tell me what's in that letter," I said.

She was in bed drinking her first cup of tea. I thought how lovely she looked with her brown hair down over her shoulders and wished I had a hint of her beauty. She set her cup on the tray. "Figchen," she said, "if you think you're so smart, *you* tell *me* what the letter says."

Feeling like a small child, I left her room to think further on the matter. After lunch, I returned with a piece of paper folded in half. On it I'd written eleven words.

"What is it now, Figchen?" she asked.

The drapes were pulled open. Low winter sunlight slanted across the floor and onto the velvet chair where she now sat. Her maid was brushing her hair.

I unfolded the paper. In a steady voice I read, "*The omens agree that Peter the Third my husband shall be.*" It had been a wild guess, but when I looked up at her, her face had gone pale. She waved her arm to dismiss her maid. When the door closed, she turned to me.

"How did you know?" she demanded.

If I revealed that it was merely guesswork, she might call me stupid. So I said nothing. A moment passed.

"All right then," she said with a sigh of exasperation. "In two days you, I, and Papá leave for Berlin to meet with King Frederick. He will be studying you, Figchen. Our family's honor and fortune depend on how you handle yourself. Since you are not beautiful, you must be charming and clever."

I tried to swallow. "How long will we be gone, Mother?"

She leaned forward, taking my chin in her hand. "You must tell no one what I'm about to say, not your brother, not even Mademoiselle. Understand?"

I nodded. Was she afraid that if others knew the truth, they might convince me to run away, thereby spoiling her scheme?

"*If* the King approves of you" — she emphasized the word "if" — "then you and I shall be driven by sleigh out of Prussia, all the way to St. Petersburg, to meet with Empress Elizabeth. We will travel under assumed names so no one will try to kidnap you. She has selected *you*, my poor ugly daughter, to be Peter's fiancée. Unless you spoil things, the two of you will marry and one day rule all of Russia. Twenty million subjects will bow to you, Figchen."

At this my mother smiled.

Papá's Warning

Mother's words stung. It hurts to be reminded that I'm not pretty.

But her report thrilled me. Russia! The duke's letter did

33

not contain an official marriage proposal, just an invitation to see the empress, but it has given my mother hope for the future of our family. She has always wanted to be related to *real* royalty.

She is telling everyone that our trip is nothing more than a friendly visit with King Frederick in Berlin, that we shall return here to Zerbst in a few weeks.

This morning when I was at my desk studying, Papá came into the room. He leaned into the wide sill, using it as a seat. I could see from his frown that he was troubled.

"What is it, Papá?"

He took a deep breath, then his face softened and he regarded me with tenderness. "Russia is a barbarous country, my daughter," he began. "If you displease the empress she can order your tongue to be cut out and send you to Siberia — the coldest, cruelest place on earth — like she did to Countess Anna Lopukhina. As you and I sit here, the countess is starving to death under terrible conditions. Nevermore will she gossip."

My father lowered his voice. "Listen carefully to me, my dear. Never argue with royalty. Never confide in your maids or ladies. And never meddle in government affairs lest the Senate resent you. You must try to please everyone. Figchen, if you remember anything at all, remember this:

Anything you say in the Russian court could be misunderstood and then used against you."

I set my pen down. "What do you mean?"

He looked out the window. From his coat pocket he brought out a pamphlet, then set it on the sill. "It's important you read this," he said, patting the cover. "It's by a German theologian, explaining the errors of the Orthodox religion."

"I'm listening, Papá."

"Figchen, the empress will force you to adopt her religion, as she did Charles-Peter. She had him baptized last year in an Orthodox rite, so now he is Grand Duke Peter Feodorovich, heir to the Romanov dynasty. Most likely she will change your name, too. Her beliefs are far from the simplicity and truth of our Lutheran faith."

"I will lean on God for understanding," I said.

Papá smiled. "You are brave, my daughter. If you end up marrying the nephew of this woman, life is going to be extremely difficult. She is renowned for her cruelty. And if she lives into old age, you will be under her thumb all those years. Your youth will be spent waiting and waiting. Indeed, you will need God's help."

I jumped up from my seat to hug my father. His shirt had the comforting smell of pipe tobacco. He crushed me in his embrace, as if to never let me go. As he held me, I wondered what it would be like to be so far away from home with a new name, a new language, everything foreign.

At that moment I wanted to remain his little girl forever, never to leave the security of his peaceful realm.

Mother had neglected to say it might be decades before I would inherit the Russian throne, *decades*.

Zerbst — The Packing Has Begun

When Freidrich saw my trunk open, he hugged me fiercely.

"I'll never see you again," he cried.

"It's not true, Freddy," I said. "Berlin is only a few days away, I'll be back soon." I hated lying to him. My little brother is my closest friend. But somehow he had learned the truth and would not be comforted.

Even Mademoiselle left my room this evening in tears.

My trunk has nothing lovely inside. Wool stockings and underskirts, head scarves, white blouses, my colorful vest and hat that I wear at Festival, this diary and some extra quills and ink. I'm also taking my German Bible. The verses I've memorized over the years are underlined in red.

As brave as I felt a few days ago, I don't feel so now. All correspondences from the empress to my parents have come through King Frederick. Now he'll be evaluating me to see if I'm fit to marry into the Russian imperial family. My throat is dry at the thought.

Did I hear Mother correctly when she said it would take five weeks to reach St. Petersburg?

Five weeks . . . in sleighs across the frozen plains!

Berlin

So much has happened in the last few days.

Saying good-bye to Mademoiselle was wrenching. How we both wept! Freddy's lip turned down before he burst into tears and ran from the hallway where our luggage was stacked. Ulrike was in her nurse's arms, unaware of the commotion. I kissed my sister's plump little hand, then turned for the waiting carriage.

It was the tenth of January. I did not look back.

Evening, It's Snowing Out

Now I am sitting in a lavish upstairs suite in the palace of King Frederick II of Prussia. A maid stands at the door ready to wait on me. This is the second day I've remained in here, taking meals by myself brought in on a tray. The king has sent messages, beseeching me to join him at his table, but Mother keeps telling him I am ill.

The reason she's lying?

I have nothing to wear!

After seeing the richness of His Majesty's court, Mother is ashamed of my wardrobe.

"He cannot see you this way," she said.

Day Three in Berlin

Only when King Frederick asked Mother if I was a feeble child or weak-minded did she finally break down and confess the truth.

Moments ago, maids brought in a gown belonging to the king's sister. It was so heavy with layers of brocades and satins and with jewels sewn along the outer seams that it took two of them to carry it.

As I write this, a lady is pinning up my hair, another just fastened a pearl-and-jade necklace around my neck — how cold the gems feel on my bare skin! A younger girl is fitting my feet into shoes, which is why my penmanship jolts here and there. Without looking down I can feel that these shoes are of the finest soft leather.

The maids are approaching me with the blue gown. Fur from a silver fox is around the neckline and at the wrists. . . . Oh, it is beautiful.

Mother is pacing the room and has just told me to put away my journal.

Before Bed

By the time I reached the wide landing at the top of the staircase, holding my head as high as I possibly could, it had been three hours of getting dressed — three hours! On the way down the stairs, Mother walked behind me, now and then jabbing my back with her finger to make me stand up straight. It is hard not to slouch with such a heavy dress hanging from my shoulders.

I found myself being led into the queen's antechamber by a tall, elegantly dressed man. His pants were blue velvet buckled at the knee, his stockings white. He wore black high-heeled shoes, which clicked along the inlaid floor as we progressed down the corridor.

To my surprise, everyone we met — ladies' maids, couriers, servants — bowed at our passing. I recognized Prince Ferdinand of Brunswick because he often visits my parents. When he made a sweeping bow with his arm and said, "Your Highness," only then did I understand who was escorting me: the king himself!

Suddenly, I felt too nervous to speak.

The king is tall with an imposing dignity. His wig was powered white and with ringlets to his shoulders. When he bent down to kiss my hand, I could see the hair was crawling with fleas. It smelled of spicy pomade.

Will write more after I find another candle. . . .

To Continue . . .

At dinner, again to my surprise, I was seated *next* to the king. Papá was elsewhere, heading his own table, and I could see Mother at another location with bewigged ladies. From the pinched look on her face I could tell she was angry not to be included in the royal circle.

Through the many courses, King Frederick asked me countless questions on just about every subject — poetry, opera, dancing, and comedy, specifically Molière's play *Le Bourgeois Gentilhomme.* (Fortunately, Mademoiselle and I had recently read it together!) At first, I felt too timid to speak my mind and couldn't imagine why the king was interested in my opinions, but he seemed genuinely so. By the time our second meat dish was placed in front of us, I had relaxed.

Soon we were chatting as if old friends.

Again, I looked for my mother. She and her table companions regarded me with slack jaws, as if they could not believe the King of Prussia and a fourteen-year-old girl had anything at all to say to each other.

The dinner took longer than getting dressed — four hours!

Now that I'm in my nightgown, the events of this evening are starting to sink in. His Highness whispered a secret to me during dessert — again I could smell his wig and see the vermin — that a few days from now he will be sending me back to Stettin.

But my carriage will not enter the city walls. To fool people here in Berlin, we will merely be dropping off my father. Then Mother and I will be driven east.

Into Russia.

𝔓𝔖

Tomorrow I must return the lovely gown and shoes. It reminds me of the story Mademoiselle read to me in French, about the little ash girl who was beautiful until the stroke of midnight, when her carriage turned into a pumpkin and her dress to rags.

Dear diary, when I looked into the mirror tonight, I did not see an ugly duckling. For the first time ever, my reflection showed a princess who is almost pretty.

Leaving Prussia

Mother and I are in a wretched little post house, filled with smoke from a cooking fire — it's not even an inn. She has settled onto a cot and said I may write until the candle goes out.

Oh, dear diary, I thought leaving my little brother and Mademoiselle was the hardest thing I've ever done, but not so. Several days ago as we headed north from Berlin, our carriage stopped at the village of Schwedt. It is south of Stettin on the Oder River. We stayed for a few minutes, just long enough for my papá to step down into the snow with his valise. A horseman and sleigh were waiting to drive him to our castle.

I leaned out to hug his neck and began weeping. He held me tight.

"Figchen," he said into my ear, "I will always love you. Remember to read your Bible, remember your Lutheran faith."

"I will, Papá." His tears were still on my cheek when our driver pulled away onto the village road that led to open country.

It is cold in this room, no heat. Downstairs is a tavern. Loud laughter from men who've been drinking all evening comes right up through the cracks in the floorboards.

I don't know how Mother can sleep. Her pillow is over her head. I won't tell her this, but I can see tiny white insects crawling over the cloth.

Though we've been traveling for days, this is our first rest in a bed. Our coachmen have been driving through the nights, stopping only to change horses and to let us ladies use a farmer's privy. As the trail cuts through the middle of nowhere, there are no cities to illuminate the horizon. The sky is as black as I've ever seen it, speckled with a brilliant array of stars. It's only by this starlight that our drivers can see their way.

There are four carriages in our convoy, pulled by twenty-four horses. Traveling with us are Mother's chamberlain, her lady-in-waiting, four maids, a valet, a cook, and several lackeys.

Mother's pretend name is Countess Reinbeck. She is thrilled with the secretiveness, which is the only thing that makes these hardships bearable for her. My name is so secret, she won't tell me what it is!

Now the men downstairs are singing. Alas, my candle . . .

On the Road Someplace

The landscape is white with snow as far as I can see, no mountains or hills or cities. I've lost count of time, and

Mother says I may as well stop trying. It seems that as soon as we cross into Russia, the dates will change from the Gregorian calendar to the Julian system and we will be eleven days behind Europe. Maybe this is symbolic — I don't know.

It is bitterly cold. Mother and I have furs over us, which we pull around our faces to keep the wind off. Though our carriage is covered, drafts seep in around the door and windows. A small brazier at our feet has coals but the warmth lasts barely an hour after they are replenished at each stop.

Will put away my pen for now. It is frustrating to write in a moving coach. See how the ink spilled?

Another Morning

I write quickly while the drivers are hitching up the horses.

Our bed last night was on the floor of the postmaster's own room. There was such an uproar I could not sleep, but the noise wasn't from singing or drunkenness. Both the man and his wife snored! Several children slept in their bed, among them an infant that cried off and on throughout the wee hours. In the dim firelight I could see the shadows of cats — two, three, maybe four? — creeping about. The family watchdog lay by the door. Just when I'd begin to doze off, it would erupt with a ferocious bark, then growl deep in its throat as if someone were prowling outside. It seemed that daylight would never come.

This morning Mother's attendants are cheerful and appear to be well rested. They slept in the barn with the larger animals with just hay for their beds. And Mother thought *they* would be the ones to suffer. Next time I will ask to join them, no matter how cold it might be.

The lady of the house has just offered me breakfast of a small barley loaf and cup of hot tea — how kind of her. I must put away this journal until there is not so much commotion.

Kurland

This post house is as rough as the others. Presently, I'm sitting on a footstool in front of the hearth with only a few minutes to write before once again our group boards the carriages.

Last night, a comet lit our way. It didn't move as shooting stars do, but sat in the sky close to the earth, like a bird with a long white tail. Throughout the night — once again I couldn't sleep — I kept getting up in the cold room to look out the window to watch what might happen. But the comet traveled only as the constellations do, inch by inch, hour by hour. The villagers say it's been sitting above the horizon for days and many are terrified, thinking it a bad omen.

Traveling Again

This morning our carriages returned to the road after spending the night in Mitau, a quaint town that offered us an inn without fleas. Though Mother and I shared a cot, we slept deeply and awoke feeling optimistic.

A Russian commander was there to meet us. Colonel Voejkov is now accompanying us to Riga and at this moment is sitting in our carriage on the seat next to Mother. He has a bushy mustache and red cheeks. I think he's one of the most patient men on earth because for three hours now he's been listening to Mother's complaints, how there were no post houses at all between Memel and Mitau, how her back hurts from sleeping on the floor, how the food is wretched and gives her gas, and on and on.

Colonel Voejkov occasionally glances over at me with a smile as if to say he understands women like my mother and does not blame me for her sour disposition. At least that is what I *hope* he thinks, because I'm embarrassed beyond words.

My ink has spilled again! Fortunately, Mother is too busy talking to notice dribbles on my skirt. The colonel says that in Riga there's a castle where I'll have my own bed. "And other surprises," he whispered to me in French when we climbed into this coach.

Truth be told, I am more weary than excited. Traveling for so many weeks is exhausting and monotonous. Our only baths have been cold water splashed on our faces, and there's been no time to do laundry. If I have to hear my mother say, one more time, that her soup is too thin — well, I just might scream.

As I look out the window at the endless white plains, I wonder about my brother Friedrich and our baby sister, Ulrike.

Do they miss me as much as I do them?

Does Mother even think about her other children?

Russia!
End of January 1744

At long last! We're in the city of Riga, on the Baltic Sea. I'm writing from a desk in the castle library, next to a window that looks out upon a frozen bay. There are sailing ships and fishing boats in the port, yet from here it appears they are locked in ice. A maid told me that the landmass far across the bay is Sweden, though it's not possible to see from here.

Colonel Voejkov was right about the surprises. In the carriage, Mother and I were awakened from a slumber by cannon fire — a salute to honor us! Townspeople crossed the Dvina River to meet us, and with them were the vice governor and a grand marshall of the court, whose Russian names I'm unable to pronounce or spell, so quick were the introductions. They presented us with gifts from Empress Elizabeth: long sable cloaks called pelisses, and tippets, which are sable hoods that hang over the shoulders in front, like long scarves. The most beautiful, warm furs I've ever felt upon my person!

Mother and I have our own apartments and new dresses to wear — though borrowed — while our others are being laundered. In a mirror over the mantel, I studied my reflection and was pleased with the color in my cheeks. I think I'm not as ugly as I was a few months ago.

A maid has brought in clean linens. . . . Will write more later.

Before Bed

Now our second day in Riga. After Mother and I had bathed and put on fresh clothes, we were led downstairs to a grand salon. We were greeted by trumpets, and nobles bowing before us! I felt breathless with surprise, and I could tell from Mother's red face that she was beside herself with pleasure.

"It's about time," she whispered to me when we were seated for dinner. The table was loaded with silver platters and kinds of foods I'd never seen before. Musicians dressed in elegant costume played drums, flutes, and brass horns in our honor.

All around us I heard French and German spoken, yet we are in Russia. My head is swimming with the luxury of this evening. Moments ago, a chambermaid brought in a nightgown for me, made of linen hemmed in lace, and warm slippers of rabbit fur. She has given me five more minutes to finish writing because it's late and I must sleep.

Tomorrow we set out for St. Petersburg, where the empress awaits us.

The thought makes me nervous. She is the most powerful woman in the land — she can do whatever she wants, whenever, and to whomever. What if the villagers are right, and the comet we saw is indeed a bad omen?

Aboard the Royal Sledge

There are many more days ahead of us before we reach St. Petersburg. But, oh, the comfort in which Mother and I are traveling.

This sledge — sleigh, I call it — is magnificent. It was waiting for us in Riga, sent by Empress Elizabeth. Thanks to her, we are warm in our pelisses and tippets. Scarlet drapes trimmed with silver braid hang about us, keeping out the wind, and we are reclining on a soft featherbed. There are cushions covered in fur and satin.

I can hear sleigh bells from the horses as they lope along the snowy road. The ride is smooth enough that I've been able to write in my journal without spilling ink. This luxury provided by the empress has reassured me a bit, though it's still possible she'll find fault with me and send us home.

Oh — Mother is passing me a picnic basket with our lunch. . . .

After Eating

Dear diary, I must make note of all the people in our convoy:

A squadron of soldiers in protective leather vests rides ahead of our sleigh — they're called *cuirassiers*. Also on horseback — alongside and behind us—are royal officers and two *grenadiers,* who are specialists in weapons.

In the other coaches are three cooks, eight lackeys, a butler, and a groom. Also assigned to Mother is a servant to prepare coffee, and a wine steward with his assistant. Two men — furriers — have the sole job of seeing to the care of our furs.

Traveling with us in our sleigh is the grand marshall, Monsieur Naryshkine — he spelled his name for me — who was an ambassador to London. His French is difficult to understand because of his heavy Russian accent.

I look over at Mother resting among her cushions and can see her contentment. When I said that I missed Papá and wished he were with us, she gave a small laugh and rolled her eyes.

"Do you miss him, too?" I asked.

She pulled back one of the drapes. Bright sunlight shone in, revealing the windswept plains outside. She looked out for a moment, then dropped the curtain without answering me.

There's no doubt in my mind that this journey means more to my mother than to me. For so long she has complained about my papá's poverty and lack of royal connections. All her life she has yearned for pomp, wealth, and fame.

But something in my heart says she's going to meet with great disappointment. What that might be, I can't even guess, but I'm worried for her.

Dorpat, Russia

Our convoy just passed this poor village. I say "poor" because long ago, Dorpat was one of the largest Livonian cities. Now much of what remains are burned and broken-down walls from when Peter the Great charged through with his cannons, conquering every town in sight.

This event was explained to me by Monsieur Naryshkine. He also said that Peter the Great came to the throne when he was just ten years old, with his older half-brother, Ivan.

"Ivan had the mind of an imbecile," said Monsieur.

Somehow this brother was eliminated from power, which I will ask about later. I listen carefully to these history lessons, to learn as much as possible in case Empress Elizabeth questions my interest in her country.

Something has sobered me, however.

Earlier we passed several sledges escorted by soldiers, coming from the opposite direction. Black curtains hid the people within. When I asked who might be inside, the grand marshall shook his head.

Without meeting my eye he said it was undoubtedly the Duke of Brunswick's family. Empress Elizabeth was expelling them and sentencing them to prison.

"My dear," he said, "it's just a whim of fate that you are proceeding toward a royal future while along this same road" — here Monsieur pulled aside our crimson drape to gesture outside — "a family is being sent away in disgrace."

His words made me feel sick inside. I remember Papá describing the countess who was sent to Siberia without her tongue.

A whim of fate.

The empress could get rid of *me*, too.

4 February 1744 —
On the Julian Calendar
St. Petersburg

Finally, St. Petersburg!

How good it felt yesterday to step out of the sledge onto the ground that is to be my new home. After forty days of travel, I was thrilled to have finally reached our destination. I bent over to kiss the snowy path, but Mother yanked my arm so I would stand up straight.

"Posture, Figchen," she said under her breath.

Such a beautiful city, glimmering under bright sunshine, the streets full of people celebrating a winter carnival. The city is named after the apostle Peter, who walked with Christ.

In our honor, cannons were fired from the other side of the river, from the fortress of St. Peter and St. Paul. This river — the Neva — is completely frozen, with children playing on it, slipping and sliding back and forth. Oh, how I wanted to run and join them!

As we were ushered to our apartments, a diplomat informed us that the empress and grand duke are in Moscow, more than forty-three miles south.

Truth be told, I was relieved by the delay, but Mother was furious they weren't here to welcome us.

"And after all we've been through," she said. She calmed down, however, upon seeing how many maids and ladies were at her service. Lovely dresses were waiting for both of us, along with fresh underclothes, shoes, and stockings. I have *four* ladies-in-waiting! Upon freshening up, Mother's outlook brightened. She decided we, too, need to be in Moscow, and no later than the tenth of February.

The reason? The grand duke's birthday. He will be sixteen.

"It will be smart politically," she told me while sorting

through a small chest of jewels. "It will show Her Imperial Majesty that already you are devoted to the grand duke, your future fiancé. She will be charmed by your obedience, Figchen."

Alas, tomorrow we must again return to the road. I'm tired of traveling, dear diary. How will I be able to make a good impression on the empress if I look as weary as I feel?

About Last Night's Dinner

Before I forget . . . I had never before seen an elephant but last night I saw fourteen of them! They were gifts to Empress Elizabeth from the ruler of Persia and were performing tricks for us during dinner. There were also dancing bears.

Dear diary, I will tell *you* because I can tell no one else, that this sight made me sad. Such magnificent animals prancing about with silly costumes is not how I think God intended them. The elephants wore satin capes over their backs with tiny matching hats tied onto their enormous heads. Bells were on their ankles. And the bears? Lacy ballerina skirts and bonnets!

The nobles and officials assigned to welcome us were proud of this entertainment, but I just smiled, saying nothing. From this moment forward I must be careful not to offend anyone, no matter how I feel.

Later

I'm hopeful about seeing Peter, possibly my future husband! It's been nearly five years since we met at his seaside castle. . . . Has he grown taller, stronger? Is he handsome? I do hope he is as eager as I am to meet again.

9 February 1744, Moscow

A quick moment to write before dinner.

This evening we arrived in Moscow. It was already dark, about eight o'clock, when our sleigh pulled up to the Annenhof Palace. Torches lit the snowpacked courtyard where liveried servants stood waiting for us.

Our journey from St. Petersburg took two full days, traveling even through the nights. The pace was exhausting. Mother and I were reclined on cushions with a charcoal brazier to warm our feet, a luxury compared to what the grenadiers on horseback had to endure. I can only imagine what it was like for them out in the cold wind, with only starlight to guide them.

The horses suffered, too. At least three dropped dead in their harnesses. The coachmen dragged them off the frozen road, then kept driving until the next hamlet. While the teams were being changed, peasants gathered around our entourage. When they saw me step out to use the privy, I could hear them saying to one another, "It's the grand duke's betrothed." Some even reached out to stroke my furs.

How could they not have guessed? Thirty sledges were in our convoy, with sixteen horses pulling mine. I smiled at each person who would meet my eye. If they are to be my subjects, I want them to like me.

Alas, as I write this, my stomach is whirling with nervousness. We're to meet the empress any minute! And Peter.

I hope my dress is all right. It's pink moiré, a type of silk with a watery appearance. It drapes nicely onto the floor but is tight around my waist. Thankfully, there's no hoop underneath! Those are tricky things when trying to maneuver into a chair. From the jewels offered me by a lady-in-waiting, I chose a single ruby to hang from my neck.

Oh, why am I bothering about such things now? I hear steps in the hallway. . . .

Midnight

Our supper ended just fifteen minutes ago. . . . Mother is on her bed with a damp towel over her eyes, too overwhelmed from this evening's events to talk. She said I may write as late as I like.

To begin, after finally seeing Peter it will be difficult to call him Grand Duke. He is just a scrawny boy! When he greeted Mother and me in our suite, I felt a tightening in my chest. I wanted to cry with disappointment. He is pale, his face oily with small eruptions on his forehead, and his voice is high like a girl's.

In my mind, I had imagined that he would have matured over the years. I realize now that I've been wishing for a *dashing* prince, one like the ash girl met before her coach turned into a pumpkin.

But this prince is far from mature. Though Peter was excited to see us, giving us both a warm embrace, he began complaining about everything Russian — the language, the religion, the tutors, the weather, even his aunt the empress. Oh, how he hates the Catholic popes! I found his gossip to be worrisome. He, too, could be sent to Siberia if he is not careful, and cause me to be dragged along with him.

Must I marry someone with such little discretion?

It is now one o'clock in the morning. Mother has fallen asleep atop her bed, still wearing her gown. She would not let her ladies undress her, such was her headache. I removed her shoes and covered her with a feather quilt so she won't catch a chill.

My candle is going. . . . Need to light another one. . . .

To Continue About Last Night . . .

Peter's purpose in coming to our rooms was to take us to meet the empress. He gave Mother his arm and I followed, escorted by the Prince of Hesse.

In the gallery, tall double doors swung open for Her Imperial Majesty. My heart raced with tension, my mouth was dry.

A rustling of silk announced her appearance. She stood before us in a silver gown adorned with gold lace, the hoop beneath her skirts spread wide about her. When she smiled at me and began speaking French, I was struck by her beauty. She is robust, with a full chin and large bosom. Her black hair was set high in silver combs with diamonds sparkling over her scalp. A tall black feather behind her ear appeared to be that of a raven.

Oh, how I wanted to stare at her, there was so much to take in. (I think she dyes her eyebrows black because there were little smudges at the edges.)

Earlier in the evening, the ladies who had helped us get ready said the empress has five thousand pairs of shoes and fifteen thousand dresses, each of which she will never wear more than once. There are too many hats, feathers, and gloves to count. Such is her admiration for King Louis XIV's court of Versailles, she allows only *couturiers,* dressmakers, from Paris to sew for her.

During our interview, Mother curtsied, thanking the empress for the many kindnesses and so forth. I, too, curtsied in the French manner, bowing from my waist and bending my knees (which were shaking). But I felt as shy as I had with King Frederick. At first, I merely responded to her questions in a soft voice: "*oui,*" "*non,*" "*merci, madame,*" those sorts of answers.

All about us, lining the corridors and rooms, were nobles, pages, diplomats, courtiers, ladies- and gentlemen-in-waiting, a physician — all regally dressed in silks and satins, jewels beyond my experience. It felt as if everyone were staring at me. *Would this be the royal bride?* they seemed to be asking.

Empress Elizabeth switched from French to German, speaking to us at length, often letting her eyes rest upon my face. I couldn't tell what she was thinking; however, I knew she was studying me. That my future lies in her hands is a terrifying thought.

Finally, she dismissed us, saying we must be tired from our journey — oh yes, dear diary, how my eyes were watering from fatigue! My back ached from trying to stand up straight for two hours because the empress had not invited us to sit.

Peter then joined us in our apartments, where a late supper was brought in. I was so exhausted I cannot recall one morsel of what I ate. The room was full of his court people, names and faces that appear to me now as a blur. Their voices were like talking dolls, making no sense to me at all. I do remember three dwarfs — little men dressed in velvet — who appeared to be servants. Their feet were as small as a child's.

At last, the first day and the first meeting are over with. I could cry with relief.

10 February 1744, Moscow

This morning, breakfast was brought to us on silver trays. I was delighted to have a bowl of coffee with hot milk, just like Mademoiselle used to make for me, the French way. The familiar aroma makes me miss her all the more. I ate the black bread and hard-boiled egg as if I were starving. After so many days of travel my appetite is finally returning.

Today is the grand duke's sixteenth birthday. A fête is scheduled for this evening, so Mother and I have the day to rest and gather ourselves.

It's also the first day of Lent. Lutherans celebrate this holiday with much less ceremony than the Orthodox do.

I will quietly observe what might be expected of me in the future.

Before Bed

Well, Peter may be sixteen now, but he is just a boy. He has even more toy soldiers than when I first met him so many years ago. I know this because he showed me the shelves in his apartment where they are lined up in rows according to the rank he's given them. There is also a cage with a large gray rat inside.

"General Fitzroy," he said by way of introducing me to the rodent. It wore a little red jacket and harness so that Peter can put him on a leash "to inspect the troops."

I was polite, even though I think the grand duke is out of his mind. It's hard to imagine being his wife. . . . Will he expect me to play with General Fitzroy?

But before I go to sleep . . .

The Portrait Ladies

The best part of the day was a ceremony in one of the grand halls. The empress approached Mother and me in a solemn manner. She placed around our necks the ribbon of the order of St. Catherine — it is blue satin and at least three inches wide.

Next, two of her "portrait ladies" pinned a star-shaped medal on each of our gowns, by the shoulder. I'm not sure yet what any of this means, but my heart relaxed seeing how the empress smiled at us. Apparently, she has now welcomed us into her circle.

I've learned that the portrait ladies are called this because the empress has bestowed upon them miniature portraits of Her Majesty, set in diamonds — the same kind of portrait that was sent to Mother when my baby sister, Ulrike, was born.

The ladies are permitted to wear them on their court gowns to signify their special relationship to the imperial family. I wonder if Mother brought her portrait from home and if it would be proper for her to wear it now. There's so much to learn about protocol — I don't want to risk doing the wrong thing.

PS

The dress worn today by Empress Elizabeth was brown, the color of milk chocolate, embroidered with silver. About her neck and bosom were so many jewels and necklaces, I could not discern what they were. I wanted to stare at her beautiful costume, especially knowing it was the first and last time any of us would ever see it on her.

Later, two of her chamberlains told us a secret about the empress. It is this:

When she loses her temper she beats her ladies and servants. Also, she often swoons from having drunk too much wine, and they must cut away her corsets and dress so she can vomit. Maybe this is why she never wears a gown more than once.

Papá's warning now troubles me: He said life with Her Imperial Majesty would be extremely difficult. Does that mean she will beat me, too, if I don't please her? Will she strike Peter when she learns the only soldiers he cares about are made of tin and that General Fitzroy is a rat?

13 February 1744, Moscow

So many secrets in this court! This morning, Peter whispered one that made my heart drop.

He's in love!

But not with me — she is a lady-in-waiting to the empress.

How splendid, I wanted to say. *Good for you, cousin.* But I just looked at him, lost for words.

When he said the name of this girl's mother, I thought I would faint.

Countess Anna Lopukhina.

"It's a shame," he said, "but Countess Lopukhina was caught plotting against the throne so my aunt banished her to Siberia. They used pinchers to pull out her tongue, then cut it off."

I flinched at his description and the reminder of Empress Elizabeth's cruelty.

Peter looked out the window. "Her daughter was sent away, too, so I must marry you instead, Figchen. The empress said so."

His coldness made me feel dismal. Oh, dear diary, this boy is to be my husband!

Yesterday afternoon when I told Mother about this, and about feeling sad, she grabbed my elbow and pushed me to the window.

Outside, snow was falling, blowing in drifts against the palace walls. Elegant sleighs were coming and going from the royal courtyard. There was an air of festivity among women in long furs and men in their square, fur hats.

"You can't back out now, Daughter," Mother said. "We've come much too far."

I knew she wasn't referring only to the distance and

time we had traveled — fifty days in all, from Zerbst to St. Petersburg and then on to Moscow. I looked at her face, hoping to find the right thing to say, but no words came. Tears sprang to my eyes — I'm not sure why — but so many emotions had captured me.

Unmoved by my distress, Mother said in measured words, her voice so low I could barely hear her, "Politics is your concern, my dear. Not love. If you give any sign that you're unhappy here, I will wring your neck."

I just curtsied and backed away, rubbing my arm from the pain of her grip. I will try hard to love the Grand Duke of Russia even though he seems to care nothing for me.

End of February 1744, Moscow

Russian is hard to learn! The alphabet is different — to me the letters look backwards and sideways — the P looks like an R, and the C looks like an S. But I'm applying myself every hour of every day.

I try to speak to the servants, a word here, a phrase there. Some answer me in French when they see my struggle, but I tell them I want to learn. I'm sure my accent is terrible.

Peter refuses to practice with me. He insists on responding in German and won't even try to converse in our new language. I'm frustrated that he doesn't take seriously that he and I most likely will rule Russia one day. He simply does not care! His favorite complaint is that he wants to go home.

Another irksome thing: Most days when the grand duke comes to my apartment to chat, his breath stinks of vodka.

So I will work hard without his help.

At night after everyone has gone to bed, I stay up with my candle and vocabulary list. Again and again I repeat those words aloud and try to say them in sentences. It helps to pace the room while reciting, though the floor is drafty even in my fur slippers.

An Aside

I do miss my brother Friedrich, and wonder how he is. Our baby sister is probably walking by now. Oh, I wish they were here! Ulrike would look dear wearing a little Russian cap with its festive colors.

After a Late Supper . . .

I wrote Papá a letter about my religion teacher, Father Simeon, and how he says the only difference between

Lutheranism and the Orthodox religion is the "external forms of worship." I told Papá I want to be a real Russian and so will be baptized in their church. I know this will upset him.

Another tutor who comes to me daily is Landé the ballet master from Paris. He's teaching me the court dances, but this morning I asked if I might be dismissed from exercises. I've been shivering all day, with a headache. Ate no breakfast or lunch, and just a bit of soup tonight.

Three Days Later

Mother has hurried away for a doctor, forbidding me to get out of bed.

I have a fever.

When she felt my forehead and learned I have been this way for days, she panicked. "It's not permissible for you to get sick," she said, slapping my cheek.

Oh, dear diary, I must lie down and sleep. . . .

10 April 1744, Moscow

Has it truly been more than a month since I last opened these pages?

I've been so ill, I scarcely remember the passage of

time. Mother hid you, dear diary — along with my pens and my ink jug — so I would not be tempted to strain myself, as if writing is a strain! It is the easiest, most comforting thing to do in my day. (Once again, I'm thankful she cannot read French.)

Sometime during my illness, I awoke to find the empress herself holding me in her arms. She was caressing my cheek and speaking to me in French of her new affection for me. It seems that everyone in Moscow believes the reason I became sick was because of my devotion to learning Russian. Studying late in my cold room, I caught a chill, which developed into pleurisy.

"You have won the hearts of your people," the empress said to me. Then, sitting on the side of my bed, she opened a small silver chest. Inside, on a cushion of blue velvet, was a diamond necklace and matching earrings. "For my adorable child," she said, kissing my brow.

Silently, I savored that she had called the Russians "*my* people."

Later that night, Mother tried on the jewelry and studied her reflection in the mirror, turning this way and that. As she returned them to the chest she said they were worth at least 20,000 rubles and were payment for my sufferings.

During the past twenty-seven days of my illness, the

empress ordered that the physicians bleed me. This happened at least sixteen times. Mother was enraged. She feared so much bloodletting would kill me and she made such a scene about the matter, the empress banished her from my sickroom.

There is tension between those two, I can feel it. It worries me.

I'm also worried my back may have become crooked like it did when I was young. The empress will certainly send me home if I become deformed. Mother keeps reminding me that nothing less than a "perfect specimen" will be allowed to marry into the imperial family.

A New Development

Doctor's orders are that I remain in bed, even though I'm beginning to feel better. It is torture just lying still!

One consolation is that I overhear things when resting. The ladies and others think I'm asleep and that I am deaf to their gossip.

But they're wrong.

Today, I learned that Mother is involved with some kind of court intrigue, that she is possibly spying for King Frederick — spying! How could she? Doesn't she remember what happened to Countess Lopukhina?

Apparently, when we visited the king in Berlin, not only was he studying *me*, he was also giving instructions to Mother. What exactly she's supposed to do and why, I do not yet know.

This evening I heard whispers that Empress Elizabeth is furious with my mother — this made my heart race! As I lay there with my eyes closed, breathing slowly as if asleep, Mother burst into my room weeping. By the time her ladies were able to calm her, I learned that the empress had exploded at her with angry words.

Did I hear correctly that she doesn't trust my mother and wants to send her away?

* * *

Since I'm allowed out of bed only to use the chamber pot, I've not been able to study myself in the mirror. Will I still be able to stand up straight? If my spine is curved, Mother will say I've ruined her life and our family's fortune.

Though she is mean and rarely shows affection, she is still my mother. She's the only one in this new country who is not a stranger to me. I don't know how I would be able to bear her disappointment.

21 April 1744, Moscow

My fifteenth birthday!

Looking out my windows, I can see that spring is near. The snow is melting and with each day, the sun climbs a bit higher in the sky. The flags around the palace are stiff with wind, the bare trees bending back and forth. Though it's still cold outside, the empress said I am now well enough to appear in public.

Oh, dear diary, I do not feel ready to show myself — the reflection in my mirror is dreadful! I am as thin as a skeleton and much of my hair has fallen out. My face is gaunt and pale. It grieves me to be so unattractive. As if to prove this, a chamberlain arrived a few minutes ago carrying a small silver tray. On it was a pot of rouge.

"Her Majesty wishes you to color your cheeks," he told me with a bow. When I stood there without taking the jar, he said, "It's an order, Miss."

I will do as I am told and paint myself to look better than I feel.

On a cheerful note, however, the mirrors show that my shoulders are straight and my posture is as before. I cannot put into words my relief.

When breakfast arrived an hour ago, I forced myself out of bed. A page rolled in a cart with two levels of food, enough for ten people — eggs, steak, potato pancakes, beets, orange preserves, black bread, honey, hot porridge with a pitcher of cream, and coffee. None of it looked appetizing, but the empress sent word that I am to eat, eat, eat. Another order.

The grand duke came while I was sipping my coffee.

"Figchen," he said, pulling up a stool to sit beside me, "I've been so worried about you. You're my only friend here."

Upon seeing his boyish affection, I felt guilty for thinking poorly of him all these weeks and will try harder to find good in him. It was a comfort speaking to him in our native language, although he does most of the talking. I just listen.

It's upsetting how much Russian I've forgotten since getting pleurisy — I *must* resume studying as soon as possible. I want to show the empress that I care about her country. But also I want to understand the conversations going on around me. Learning what people are saying will be like uncovering a treasure.

Am not looking forward to tonight's birthday festivities. Mother said, like it or not, I must make a show of being healthy. "Just a little while longer, Daughter, and your betrothal will be official. You will be that much closer to the throne. Smile." Once again, Mother said nothing about how many years I might remain a grand duchess while the empress ages.

I must put down my pen, dear diary. A maid is bringing a dress to me that has been taken in at the seams, to accommodate my being so thin. It is the most beautiful jade green with blue lace over the skirt.

Oh, how could I have forgotten to mention my newest gift from the empress? It's a dear little snuffbox, decorated with diamonds, that fits in my palm. The note read, "To my adorable child." Might I presume she likes me?

3 May 1744, Moscow

The empress left this morning on a pilgrimage to Troitza, one of the many monasteries in Russia. Peter said she goes there when she wants to reflect and when she must make important decisions. Because it is a spiritual journey, she likes to walk — more than sixty miles! He explained that it takes her at least a week and instead of camping along the way, a carriage follows her. When she has done walking for the day, the carriage returns her to Moscow, where she eats dinner and sleeps. Then in the morning she is driven back to the place where she stopped the day before, to resume her trek. This is repeated each evening until she reaches Troitza.

Peter told me this pilgrimage is different, however. "She is riding in her coach the entire way," he said. "She's in a big hurry for some reason; I do not know why."

He seemed nervous when telling me this but, truth be told, I am relieved she will be gone. I want to catch up on my Russian studies. Also, it will be easier to relax knowing Her Imperial Majesty is not in the palace, where she can summon me at any moment.

Before Bed

Oh, dear diary, I am not to be at ease after all!

A courier just left our rooms with a message from the empress. She has sent for Mother, Peter, and me — it is an order! Our carriage leaves in the morning.

Now, like Peter, I am wondering why she hurried to the monastery. And why is it so urgent that we come, too?

Troitza

We arrived an hour ago. Mother and I are sharing an apartment. She has lain down to rest while the maids unpack our bags.

Peter's room is down the hall.

As we stepped out of the carriage, a monk told us this monastery owns fifteen districts. He swept his arm toward the vast countryside, saying there are many thousands of serfs who farm and try to live off the land. He leaned near me to whisper. "It would be good for you to meet some of these people," he said.

I understood him to mean that these serfs might well be my subjects one day.

A chamberlain has just entered our room with instructions. He will escort Mother and me and Peter to the empress right away. I write this quickly while Mother dabs rouge on her cheeks. . . .

Near Midnight

Things did not go well this evening. In fact, I fear for my mother's life.

The grand duke and I were told to wait in the empress's antechamber while Mother went in to see her. He and I have been enjoying a playful friendship since my illness, so we were not unhappy to have been left alone.

We boosted ourselves onto a high window seat where we could look out over the farmland. At the sight of two baby goats butting their little heads, we laughed. Then Peter hit my arm as he would a sister, and I punched him back. We were still laughing when the door banged open and Count Lestocq stormed into the room. He is the empress's advisor and physician.

He marched over to where we were sitting and looked directly at me. "Pack your bags at once, German girl. You're going home to where you came from."

Peter sat up straight. "What's the meaning of this?"

"You're about to find out," said the count. Then he turned on his heel and left.

Peter and I were stunned into silence. I tried not to cry, but I felt terrified. My future had just slipped away. For some reason I had displeased Her Majesty.

Seeing my tears, Peter patted my hand. "I wouldn't be surprised if your mother is at fault. But whatever it is, you shouldn't be blamed, Figchen."

One moment, dear diary, I need to light another candle. . . .

To Continue . . .

The grand duke and I were still sitting in the window, wondering what had happened, when the door was again flung open and in came the empress, her face red with anger. Behind her was my mother, tears streaming down her cheeks.

Peter and I jumped down from the seat. My heart was pounding, for I knew something dreadful had taken place. I curtsied before the empress, bowing my head, and murmured a bit of Russian I'd been practicing:

"*Vinovata, Matuska.*" I am at fault, ma'am. I glanced up at her, of course not knowing what I was apologizing for, only that I felt I must.

The empress's hard look softened into tenderness, and she bent down to lift me from my curtsy. She kissed my forehead. Then without a word she left the room.

At this moment, Mother is in bed and won't tell me what happened. Another of her secrets has become torture for me!

Next Day

This morning while eating breakfast in a sun parlor, I overheard two servants. They were just outside a bank of windows, sweeping a garden path while discussing the empress. Fortunately, they spoke in French.

"Two things Her Majesty hates more than anything," said one, "are deceit and disloyalty."

"Well, then," said the other, "no wonder she loathes that German woman."

As I strained to listen, I finally understood what had led up to the confrontation last night. Someone loyal to the empress has been intercepting and decoding the letters between King Frederick of Prussia and the Princess of Anhalt-Zerbst — my mother has indeed been spying!

I am sick about all this and don't know what to do.

The servants mentioned other intrigues and political problems, but I am most upset about the one involving my mother.

22 June 1744, Moscow

Another six weeks have passed since writing, and already it's summer! The trees are thick with shade, flowers line the paths and gardens. I have been wearing white cotton dresses to keep cool on my walks outside.

As you can see, dear diary, the empress did not send me home. I do not know why she changed her mind that evening at the monastery, except that perhaps upon seeing me she realized I was not involved in Mother's schemes.

I am relieved to say Mother was not sent to Siberia, nor was her tongue cut out. She is being punished, however.

The empress has forbidden her to appear at court except at the most formal events. And after my wedding she will be deported from Russia, never to return.

Another humiliation is this: In order to visit me, my

mother must have a courtier announce her. No longer can she just wander into my room to say hello. This formal ritual will always separate the two of us. She is furious and humiliated. This upsets me, too, but I must keep silent. I just hope Mother is as thankful as I am that she wasn't banished to the far north.

Since the monastery I've kept busy with my studies — language, religion, dancing, and etiquette — which is why I've neglected you, dear diary.

24 June 1744, Moscow

Three days from now I shall be confirmed in the Orthodox Church, by order of the empress. Then the following day — the feast of St. Peter and St. Paul — my cousin and I will be officially betrothed. I almost wrote that we will "celebrate our betrothal," but it will hardly be a celebration.

I don't think he looks forward to being my husband any more than I do being his wife. Lately, our friendship has deepened, but we are more like brother and sister. We have come to tease each other and appreciate that we're the same age, were raised Lutheran, and have German as our native language. I do like it when he calls me Figchen and invites me for walks in the palace gardens.

Alas, I am resigned that our marriage will not be a romantic one. It is the Russian crown I see in my future. Mother keeps reminding me that she has hoped for this since my birth.

"Almost there," she said into my ear this morning after breakfast. This was *after* she was announced by a lady-in-waiting and *after* I said that she may enter. I am still not comfortable ranking higher than my own mother, but this is how we must conduct ourselves from now on.

In the meantime, Bishop Pskov said I must fast these next three days — only water! I do not like going without food, especially now that my health has returned and, along with it, my appetite. These past two months I have eaten heartily at every meal. To my great relief, my back did not become crooked during the weeks in bed, and my cheeks are plump. I have even put away the empress's rouge pot.

26 June 1744, Moscow

My Russian is picking up again. I practice reading the doctrine aloud, again and again. Father Simeon says my pronunciation is good, but I can still hear my German accent inside my head.

Could not sleep last night from hunger. If only I were

saintly, fasting would not seem such agony. I do not understand its purpose, but am doing so to show I'm willing to obey. During my long night I got up to look out the window and was rewarded by an amazing sight.

The sky glowed with color — green, blue, purple — waves of light shimmering above the horizon, changing shape every few seconds. Such was my delight, I ran into Mother's room to wake her. But her bed was empty! She may have been down the hall playing cards with her ladies — oh, I do hope it is cards and not intrigue.

27 June 1744, Moscow

Cannot stop thinking about food. I keep praying and asking God for strength, but I just feel light-headed and weaker by the hour.

Peter said the empress is going to change my name because she thinks "Sophie" is soiled. It reminds her of another Sophie, the half sister of Peter the Great, who conspired against him and was banished to a convent. It was such a scandal, the empress does not want any of it attached to her court.

I wonder if Mother was aware of this bit of history when she chose my name at my christening.

Last night I again got out of bed to sit by the open

window. From far off came the hoot of an owl, then another answering it. The breeze was so soft, I wished for wings to fly into the night, to follow the colors in the dark sky.

In one way, hunger has given me a gift: Without fasting, I would not have noticed the northern lights, the most beautiful display I've ever seen. Unlike the comet in Kurland, I watched the sky until I could no longer keep my eyes open.

A Letter from Papá

My dear father is crushed that I'm giving up my Lutheran faith. But he's more unhappy about an order from the empress, delivered to him by courier at our castle in Stettin.

"I am forbidden to set foot in Russia," he wrote me. He was told *not* to attend my confirmation and that he will *not* be invited to my wedding. I don't understand why, only that Her Imperial Majesty wishes it so.

And to make matters worse, he's asked Mother to return as soon as possible because my brother is ill.

How my heart grieves — only now am I realizing I may never again see my beloved Papá or even my brother and sister. And if Mother leaves, I'll be here alone, without any family or friends. Peter will be the only person from my homeland.

At the last page of his letter, Papá drew a picture of our palace courtyard in Stettin. On one of the tower walls is a clock that is molded like a face. When it chimes on the hour, the half hour, and quarter hour, its huge eyes roll about and the mouth opens wide. How I used to laugh as a child when Papá held me in his arms, pointing to it. It was one of our favorite things to do together, to go say hello to the clock.

28 June 1744, Moscow

Alone at last!

It is late afternoon and I am in a room on the top floor of the Kremlin, an ancient castle built for royalty. It is so high up that people walking in the courtyard below appear as small as insects. The desk where I am sitting is by a window, ajar to let in a breeze, its curtain fluttering against my hand. Finally, I am beginning to relax.

Oh, where to begin?

Today's events were so exhausting I asked to be excused from the state banquet, which is beginning at this very moment. Even though it is in my honor, the empress said I might come here to rest.

This morning, maids awakened me before dawn. A tray

was set by my bed, with bread and a bowl of soup to break my fast. I was ravenous and could have eaten five times that amount. Even now my stomach feels hollow.

Next, I was taken to the empress's apartment to dress. My gown was identical to hers, scarlet trimmed with silver, the material quite heavy against my skin, One of her ladies brushed my hair up into a white ribbon, then gave my cheeks a hard pinch to bring out the color — why she didn't use the rouge pot, I do not know.

In the mirror I had the look of a surprised girl wearing grown-up clothing. I am certain I am not as ugly as before, but no one said I was pretty or even complimented me.

Our procession from the palace to the church was watched by lines of people standing to our left and right. The chapel was crowded, and there were so many eyes upon me. At the door I was told to kneel upon a square cushion, then proceed before the altar. The woman appointed to be my godmother was someone I had never met, the head Abbess of the Novodevichi Convent. She was hunched over with age — at least eighty years old — and spoke not a word to me.

Only on my way up to this room an hour ago did I learn from a maid that ladies from every rank and every noble family had begged the empress for this honored role, to be my godmother. What they're supposed to do, I do not know, but the abbess was chosen because she is pious, not political.

More later . . . a groom has brought in a tray with supper. Oh, am I famished!

The Ceremony

It would give me another headache to repeat everything that happened, so I will be brief.

At the altar I read the fifty pages of the creed, then recited my confession of faith. I spoke slowly, trying to pronounce the Russian as carefully as possible. This effort helped keep me calm. But, oh, my throat was so dry I grew hoarse.

When I finished, I looked up to see almost everyone in tears. The empress herself held a handkerchief to her cheek. She gazed at me with affection, nodding her approval.

Then she led me to communion, given by a priest with a long white beard. I know this is a sin, but at the taste of bread and sip of wine, all I could think about was my hunger! And the itchiness of my dress — lace along an inside seam was bothering me to distraction. I pray God will forgive me for not paying attention during such a holy event.

I also pray that Papá will forgive me. I have done exactly what I promised him I would *not* do: abandon the simplicity of my Lutheran roots.

Right now I'm in my nightgown, my face by the window to feel the fresh air. A lady-in-waiting told me the reason it doesn't open all the way is to prevent someone from leaning out too far and falling to his death. Or jumping. It's happened before, she said, but I was afraid to ask for details.

I have turned my attention to a small silver box on the table where I write. The lid clicks just so when opened, a pleasant sound revealing the treasure within: a diamond hanging from a delicate gold necklace with a brooch to match, gifts from the empress. She presented the box to me this morning after the ceremony, as if to further welcome me to her family.

A New Name

I am now Catherine Alexeyevna, Grand Duchess of Russia, Her Imperial Highness. The title sounds odd because I still feel as if I'm Figchen, Princess Sophie Augusta Fredericka of Anhalt-Zerbst.

It will take getting used to.

Catherine is the name of the empress's mother. Even

though Russian tradition is that the father's name be added to the child's, my papá's has been omitted. He is just a soldier with no royal blood, and worse — a Lutheran.

For this reason I feel sad tonight.

Alas, dear diary, it is late and I must put you away and go to sleep. Tomorrow is another big day, my engagement to be married. I hope my heart will feel *something* for Peter besides sisterly fondness.

29 June 1744 — St. Peter's Day, Moscow

I am officially the grand duke's fiancée.

Early this morning a chamberlain brought me a small portrait of the empress the size of a cookie, framed in diamonds. Then moments later, another chamberlain entered my suite, this time carrying a portrait of Peter, also encircled in diamonds. In this painting he wears a white wig curled up to his ears. I must say this likeness makes him look handsome.

I carried the portraits to the window to better see them. The diamonds sparkled as I held them in the sunlight, admiring their beauty and pondering the events that brought me to Russia from a small German village. Even in my girlish fantasies I never dreamed of owning such exquisite jewelry.

A maid fastened the portraits to the front of my dress. When the pins poked through the fabric and pricked my skin, I flinched but said nothing. The ladies fixing my hair exclaimed that the diamonds sitting so close to my face brought a certain beauty to my eyes. Their praise helped me stand taller, truly!

Soon Peter came to my apartment to escort me to the empress. He smiled like an old friend, giving me a dainty kiss on each cheek. I felt hopeful by his affection and took his arm with a new confidence. We worked our way through the maze of corridors and halls, our every step watched by nobles, court people, and servants who had come out to witness the event.

How will I ever get used to so many people staring at me?

The empress awaited us on the landing of a wide stairway, her proud head adorned with her crown, and her imperial mantle across her chest. The sight of her imposing figure — tall and arrayed with jewels — made my stomach flutter. This was the most powerful woman of the largest country in the world standing before us, ready to formally declare *me* her heir.

If only she would smile, I thought, *then I could relax.*

But she was like a rock. It was almost too much to bear. My knees felt weak, I forced myself to stand straight. How

I wanted to stare at the empress's magnificent costume and all the gems set within her crown, but dared not. From just a glance, I noticed that among the diamonds and rubies, there was an emerald the size of a coin.

Dear me, this candle is a puddle. . . .

To Continue About the Betrothal . . .

Where did I leave off? Oh, yes . . .

Standing at the top of the grand staircase with Empress Elizabeth were eight major generals, their uniforms decorated with colorful patches and medals. Their arms were clenched to their chests as they held up a massive silver canopy that sheltered the empress. At our approach, she turned to lead us down the flight of stairs, the grand duke behind her and I behind him. My mother was allowed to follow at a distance, then behind her came numbers of princesses and ladies according to their ranks.

Such a swishing of dresses and *click-clicking* of shoes along the marble floor! I dared not look over my shoulder to see my mother's face, but I imagined she was beaming with importance.

So slow were the empress's steps, it seemed to take forever to reach the bottom of the staircase. Finally, we were outside, crossing the vast square as if on a solemn march —

still I could hear the footsteps and swish of satin from every lady behind us. All along our path, soldiers stood at attention. The sun was hot.

Empress Elizabeth walked in the shade of her canopy, the only person among the throngs to be protected from the heat.

In the cool entryway of the Cathedral of the Assumption, the robed clergy greeted us with nods of the head and brief comments, very little of which I understood. The empress took my hand and Peter's, then led us to the center of the church where there was a platform carpeted in velvet. Waiting for us there was the archbishop.

Dear diary, I can scarcely put into words how torturous this ceremony was — it lasted four hours! Not allowed to sit, it was impossible for me to pay attention. Not only was the Russian language a mumble of words, but my gown itched terribly. The weight of its heavy fabric made my shoulders ache.

Also, the incense a priest was waving about in a silver ball made me sneeze. How my eyes watered trying to blink away more sneezes! With so many people watching, I dared not raise my sleeve to my nose. Another distraction was hearing the name "Catherine" instead of "Figchen" or "Sophie." It made me want to look around. Who was this new girl everyone seemed to know except me?

Oh, there was so much I wanted to take in! The ornate decorations in the church, the tall ceilings and alcoves decorated with statues, the silver bowls and candlesticks, the paintings, the priests in their gold robes and long beards, their musical chants. Truth be told, I could not tell whether their words were Greek or Russian.

The empress stood with us as the archbishop pronounced us betrothed, then she exchanged our rings. At that moment, by what must have been a prearranged signal, we could hear from outside the booms of cannons being fired and the ringing of bells throughout Moscow from all the city's churches — five hundred, I was told.

The First Banquet

Our midday meal was a disaster.

Peter and I were dining with the empress in the Granovitana Palace. Our table of honor was on a raised dais where we could look out over the scores of guests seated around the hall. I was still so overwhelmed and numbed by the ceremony, I could eat only a bite of bread. And my attempts to make small talk in Russian were failing because my mind had gone blank. It was all I could do to keep back tears of frustration.

The problem was made worse when Mother came up to

our table, demanding to sit with us. I could not believe her audacity. I wanted to melt with humiliation.

"As mother of the Grand Duchess Catherine," she said, "I am entitled to such privilege." There was that strange name again, *Catherine*! — how quickly she had adopted my new identity.

Peter, the grand duke, looked at her with an arched eyebrow. Though I was furious at my mother for her rudeness, I was equally mad at him for then rolling his eyes. He clearly does not have the skills of a diplomat because he did nothing to try to ease any of our discomfort. He continued to eat his soup as would a child, not even using his handkerchief to dab his chin.

"Well?" said my mother when there was no response.

Finally, the empress motioned to the master of ceremonies, who appeared immediately at her side.

"Arrange a very special place for madame," she said, indicating my mother.

That the empress did not even say mother's name or title was evidence to me of her displeasure.

The man bowed, then bade my mother to follow him. I do not think she would have smiled so broadly had she realized the special place was in a private room all by herself!

A glass window separated her from the dais where we sat. It pained me to see my mother eating alone at a large table, trying to hold her head high, no doubt struggling against the tears I myself felt. I worry that her vanity might lead to a worse isolation.

Siberia has no window through which she would be able to watch the rest of us.

After that embarrassment, my headache would not leave. The evening banquet passed, then the ball. I remember dancing the minuet with Peter, grateful for my lessons with Monsieur Landé.

But at that late hour I felt suffocated by the crowds and the orchestra. To me the violins sounded like bees buzzing, not a waltz. Even one of the servants guarding the doors fainted from the heat. When they carried him away, his powdered wig slipped off his head and onto the floor. The other servants were dressed like him, in the same French style: breeches with white stockings, and black high heels.

Before Bed

Even now, dear diary, with the day's events behind me, I am still exhausted. And confused. There are too many new rules and rituals. Though I can speak short phrases in Russian, and I understand *some* people when they speak slowly, the language is still a mystery. To me, their words sound like dogs barking!

Then regarding Papá . . . does it truly matter *how* I worship, as long as it is *Christ* I worship?

Oh, my tears won't stop. Mother is in her apartment celebrating my new status with her ladies, although I wonder what she has told them about her "special table." A Russian girl about twelve years of age has folded down the coverlet of my bed. Now she is bringing me a pretty nightgown, a soft yellow with blue trim. I pray she will not report that I've been crying.

The words of dear Mademoiselle Babette come to me now:

"Get some sleep, Figchen. Tomorrow will look better through fresh eyes."

So, I am setting down my pen and closing these pages.

P.S.

Alas, I can't leave you, dear diary, not yet. Now that the maids have gone to their own quarters and I am finally alone, I want to confess a sadness.

I do not feel like a "Catherine."

It's dreadful of me to complain about this, considering all that has been given me these past weeks. But I *do* wish I could have chosen my new name, something familiar. Perhaps Christianne, after my papá, Christian, or even

Ulrike, after my sister. But "Catherine" feels like I'm wearing a dress that is scratchy and too big.

On another matter, I hope I do not have to wear the grand duke's ring every day! It is so heavy, it slips around my finger and the stones snag the cloth of my skirt. Before she returned to her apartment tonight, Mother took my hand and gave my ring a good look, saying it is worth 12,000 rubles. The one I bought Peter — from my new expense account — cost 14,000 rubles.

"It is obvious you have better taste, my dear," she said.

I surprised myself by rushing into her arms. At first she resisted, but when I didn't let go, she returned my embrace, even brushing her cheek against mine as she used to do when I was small.

How I wished she had not angered the empress and that we could visit each other whenever we want, without maids reporting our conversations.

5 July 1744, Moscow

Russia is beautiful in summer. The nights are warm and full of pale light. The mysterious colors that shimmer in the sky after sunset make me feel hopeful for some reason. Their unexpected beauty stirs something inside me.

My days are not quite so lonesome now that I

understand more of my new language. I practice with every lady-in-waiting, tutor, butler, and gardener I see, and they are all patient with me, even gently correcting my many mistakes with grammar.

I have grown to love this country, though I have still seen so little of it. Even the religion — with its rituals and ornate decor — brings comfort. Papá would be shocked to know how quickly I have taken to it.

20 July 1744, Moscow

My studies have been devouring all my time, but with pleasure. A fortnight has passed without my writing in these pages, but I am doing so now to report that my peaceful summer is being interrupted.

The empress has ordered us to follow her to yet another monastery! This one — the Monastery of the Caves — is the oldest in Russia. It is many miles south of here in the Ukraine, by the city of Kiev.

Already maids are packing. The journey will take at least three weeks, then another three weeks to return. Oh, dear diary, summer will be over by then. How I dread sitting in a carriage all that time and camping by night. I have become spoiled by my soft bed and my evening bath. Will I find time along the way to study?

Peter is as excited about this trip as a boy with nothing to do — anything to break the monotony of his lessons. A main difference between us is that I love to learn and I want to become a true Russian. He's indifferent.

"I'm German," he told me again this morning. "And I shall remain so forever."

On the Road to Kiev

We are camped along a stream for two nights to rest the horses, so at last I have time to write. I am sitting in the shade of our tent, on the ground where a trail of ants is marching by my foot. Everywhere I look is rolling plains, yellow from the sun and lack of rain. We have passed dozens of tiny villages that seem nothing more than clusters of huts. Each time we stop, the peasants come out of their poor dwellings to offer us black bread and salt.

I am touched by this symbol of hospitality, yet embarrassed. They have so little, and I have so much. What can I give or do to make their lives easier? None of my companions seem to care, least of all Peter.

"Let the empress worry about her people," he said when I mentioned my concern. "She is going to be on the throne for a while. We are just the ducal couple."

I've been thinking about his comment. How is it that

so much honor is bestowed on us, yet no power to help those who someday will be our subjects? Harsh as this may sound, it could be *years* before the empress dies.

Perhaps the monk at Troitza Monastery understood this when he said I should visit the serfs.

* * *

Unlike our previous journey, the empress's caravan left days *after* ours. A courtier who caught up to us this evening said there have been some "unfortunate incidents" that will delay her further. As a result, she is in a foul mood and has ordered several people in her entourage to be exiled — banished to Siberia! This news put a twist in my stomach. One tiny misstep on my part and I, too, could be sent away.

This courtier also told us that when we reach the Ukraine we are to stop in the city of Koseletz and wait for the empress there. She's traveling with nearly three hundred people and apparently is transporting much of her furniture, kitchen equipment, cooks, laundresses, a seamstress, and so on. It is as if a small city is moving with her — even livestock so the chef will have fresh meat. At each relay station between Moscow and Kiev, there are eight hundred horses waiting for the empress's use.

This is such an immense country and everything is at

her disposal, even Peter and I. No matter what, we must do as she says.

Next Day

This morning before sunrise I bathed in the stream. Everyone was still asleep except for a maid who was starting our breakfast fire. As I was rising from the cold water, dripping wet, she brought over a white tablecloth to wrap around my shoulders.

While I was dressing in my tent, I heard two people arguing outside the thin canvas wall. Their language was German.

"You are impudent as well as an idiot," said a woman I recognized as my mother.

"And you, madame, are *zemleroika*." There was no mistaking Peter's voice and that he had used Russian to call my mother a shrew — they were fighting! But why?

I must continue this later, as the horses are being harnessed for another long day.

2 August 1744, Koseletz

For several days we've been staying in a mansion built by Count Rasumovski. It is luxurious, though crowded — Mother and I must share a room, and our ladies sleep on cots in the antechamber. While we wait for Empress Elizabeth to arrive, we rest, walk through the gardens, and relax over quiet dinners. I've even been able to keep up with my Russian studies.

An unpleasant event has me quite upset, however.

The grand duke and I are learning to enjoy each other's company. Sometimes we play hide-and-seek among the furniture or we play tag outside with the young servants. After our game yesterday, Peter caught up to me in my apartment. He began jumping and clapping as he usually does when he wins.

Well, in doing so, he accidentally bumped a small chest of Mother's valuables that had been on a stool. His sleeve caught the open lid and tipped over the box, spilling everything to the floor: rings, necklaces, bracelets, brooches, a silver bookmark.

Mother had been writing a letter at the nearby table. She was furious and grabbed Peter's arm, yelling at him, "You did that on purpose, you wicked child!"

Peter pulled away from her and in Russian said, "Madame, you have the breath of a dog." I cringed, hoping she wouldn't recognize the word for dog — *sobaka* — but she certainly understood his tone. When she lunged for him I rushed over. Trying to calm her, I spoke softly in our native tongue. Her response was to slap *me*!

I burst into tears.

Seeing my distress, Peter hurried to my side and put his arm around me, further accusing my mother with words I won't repeat here. Their voices sounded like magpies'.

Two surprises consoled me, however:

One, that the grand duke defended me as a friend. Two, that his Russian was fast and furious. He may protest learning our new language, but he knows more than he lets on.

Before Bed

Our window is open. I can hear crickets outside in the grass and the splashing of a nearby stream. I have this late hour to myself because Mother is downstairs playing cards with the count and his friends.

I tried hard all day to be an ambassador between her and my fiancé, but both are determined to dislike each other. I don't know what to do.

As I look out at the starlight and a crescent moon, I realize I feel closer to Peter than ever before. My affection for him is sisterly, but genuine. At least we will be friends when we marry.

I realize also that my future is with him and this vast country, not with my mother. Though I will continue to show her respect, my efforts will go toward Russia and pleasing the empress.

One question that bothers me . . . When will our wedding take place? No one seems to know.

An Afternoon Sitting by the River

Have lost track of the dates, but can report that the empress arrived several days ago with her entourage. We have been waiting three weeks for her!

Now that Her Imperial Majesty is here, the evenings have become wild with dancing and gambling, and the ladies-in-waiting compete with one another for the most elegant gowns. The uproar of their laughter and music lasts long into the wee hours. Only when everyone has drunk too much wine am I able to slip away to my room unnoticed.

This morning during breakfast, a page came into the sun parlor with a message from the empress. Tomorrow we leave for Kiev. At sunrise, the entire court — all our wagons, carriages, servants, soldiers, horses, and livestock — will gather itself for yet another journey.

I feel like a vagabond, a bird without a nest. How am I to put down roots in Russia if we keeping moving from place to place? The only good I can find in this upheaval is that I am able to see more of Russia and her people.

As an aside, the weather is even warmer here than in Moscow. An ambassador told me we are nearly as far south as Paris, a city that he said is stiflingly hot during summer.

30 August 1744, Kiev

Yesterday the empress, Peter, and I crossed the river Boris-thene on a wooden bridge, by foot. Some of the beams were quite far apart, with a view down into the water. I stepped carefully all the way across, nervous about falling in, but the empress walked with her head high, as if she had done this many times. I had not realized this journey was yet another pilgrimage for her.

The clergy, who carried banners, icons, and a large silver crucifix, had met us at the outskirts of the city to lead us to the Pecherski Monastery. Priests and monks were singing the liturgy, their voices like a low hum. The church there has an image of the Virgin on one of its walls, said to have been miraculously painted by Saint Luke. Worshippers come from all over, hoping the sight of the Holy Mother will bring a miracle for them.

We followed the Cross, a slow and somber procession.

The sun beat down on our heads. I was miserable in my dress, which was heavy and too tight at the waist, and my shoes had filled with sand when I stumbled into soft dirt. I regretted not being able to have refreshed myself upon leaving our coach, but as I complained silently I noticed the crowds watching us — beggars holding out their palms, and peasants with wives and children. They were all along our route, hundreds upon hundreds. Also I noticed scores of pilgrims, smiling at us and singing hymns, apparently having walked for miles and days to reach this sacred site.

The spectacle made me uneasy because most of the people were dressed in rags, and their faces were thin.

I wonder how Her Imperial Majesty feels seeing her subjects starving and in such poverty. Her eyes revealed only a fierce determination, but to do what I do not know.

When we stepped inside the cool sanctuary of the church, it took a while for my eyes to become adjusted to the dim light. I was amazed by its magnificent finery — statues covered in gold, silver, and jewels, candles and incense, tapestries. The stained-glass windows were high up in the eaves where pigeons roosted. I could hear the flapping of their wings when the tall wooden doors opened.

8 September 1744, Kieb

Every day the grand duke and I accompany the empress to visit one church after another, as well as the convents. It is tiring to walk for so many hours in the sun with only a slight breeze coming off the river. We walk four abreast: Her Imperial Majesty, then Peter, then me, then my mother. Crowds follow us and stare.

Mother is bored by these religious exercises, but she is thankful to be included. Neither the empress nor my fiancé speaks to her, however.

When we learned there are catacombs under the city, Peter and I asked if we could explore them. It would be interesting and give us relief from the heat.

"Absolutely not," said the empress. "The catacombs are evil and damp."

Though the afternoons are hot, I can tell autumn will be here soon enough. Day by day the sun moves a bit lower in the sky. The night air is cool enough that when I step outside I wrap a shawl over my shoulders.

Am tired and ready for bed. For supper I ate alone in my room, beet soup with black bread dipped in oil. One of the maids brought me a wafer frosted with sugar.

Another Thought

To the peasants, their empress is pious. But at nightfall when they return to their huts, most of them are unable to see that she is quite the opposite once the sun sets.

Her Majesty enjoys hosting dinners, dances, card games, and concerts. The other evening we attended a theatrical performance outdoors, our royal "box" an open-sided tent. There were choirs, a ballet, then a monologue, followed by a stage play. But this play dragged on for so long that the empress finally ordered them to stop two hours after midnight!

Fireworks were the finale. The sky lit up with color. Unfortunately, the explosions so frightened the horses that they took off running, creating a mess of torn banners and flags, broken chairs, and spilled vats of wine. I do not know if anyone was hurt, but I did hear a woman weeping.

Next Day

At breakfast this morning, a porter announced that the entire Russian court is heading north, back to Moscow. The reason?

Empress Elizabeth is bored.

Moscow, I Am Not Sure of the Date

Forgive me, dear diary, for not writing all these weeks. Twenty-two days in the jolting coach . . . I just could not bring myself to again describe the forlorn villagers.

Evening

The grand duke and I have resumed our childlike amusements. This afternoon we were in his suite with several of the younger staff and his three dwarfs. Always looking for something new to do, Peter suggested we use the lid of his harpsichord for a slide. So we removed it from the keyboard, then propped it against a bureau with cushions below.

I admit it was fun, although I had trouble keeping my skirt from flying above my knees. Our shrieks of merriment brought several chamberlains to investigate, but they did not stop us. Two hours of this wore me out. I kissed Peter on the cheek and returned to my apartment for a rest.

It was a silly sport, but I want to please my fiancé. It seems that the more I play games with him, the more he takes me into his confidence. As yet, he shares no thoughts about the day he and I might rule Russia. Each time I mention wanting to help the serfs, he changes the subject, preferring to gossip about the servants and other intrigues.

Early October 1744, Moscow

Leaves are dropping from trees, swirling like orange and yellow butterflies. It's so refreshing to be outside in the cool air and to see such beauty. It reminds me of the pleasant autumn days of my childhood.

But I can scarcely enjoy this day because the empress is furious with me! Oh, dear diary, I can't bear being under such constant scrutiny — my every move is evaluated. What happened is this:

With my new allowance I sent some money to Papá, to help care for my brother Friedrich. Also with the money, I purchased a few new dresses — measured and sewn for me by a local dressmaker — as well as shoes, gloves, and stockings, small gifts for the maids. My betrothment ring for Peter was the biggest expense.

Well, this evening at the theater, I noticed across the stage, in the box opposite mine, that the empress was having a heated discussion with Count Lestocq. I could tell from her expression that she was angry. Moments later, the count made his way along the balcony and — at the box where I was seated with the grand duke — yanked aside the curtain that afforded our privacy.

"You wasteful thing," the count said to me, "spending money like you are a queen when you're merely a duchess.

Already you are in debt for seventeen-thousand rubles. Who do you think you are, anyway?"

My mouth dropped open, but I was unable to speak.

He continued. "Even when the empress was your age she did not waste other people's money. She was frugal, respectful. So should you be." Then he stormed out, causing the curtain to swing from its overhead hooks.

Then the worst happened. Peter turned on me — my friend! He gestured in a way that I am sure the empress witnessed from across the theater.

"Yes, indeed, Figchen," he said. "I am in complete agreement with my aunt, that you spend too much." His criticism was such a surprise, I felt crushed. Now I realize he finds it more important to side with Her Majesty than to be my friend.

When I returned to my apartment, too upset to remember anything about the play, my despair deepened. Mother chastised me for the same thing.

"Figchen," she said, "I am not surprised by your foolishness. This is what happens when a girl of fifteen has too much freedom."

I am so frustrated!

How can I learn what is expected of me if no one explains? I did not know I must follow a budget. I'm confused, because in addition to the purses of coins, I have received jewelry and other precious things from the empress — sometimes as often as twice a week. Even today I received a delicate clock three inches tall, its base studded with opals.

I wish Papá were here to help me! He was right about life being difficult with Empress Elizabeth.

To bed now, before my eyes blur further. A chime down the hallway just finished announcing it is midnight.

Next Morning

I am putting my affairs in order and have asked that all my accounts be presented to me.

It is true I owe 17,000 rubles, a huge sum! I had no idea I was supposed to keep track of my spending. But the good news is, the empress gave me an allowance of 15,000 rubles, which I will use to pay off my debt. That means I owe just 2,000. I considered selling a necklace or brooch, but thought better of it.

She has not said when or even *if* she'll give me more allowance. But if she does, I can use it to pay the rest of my bills. Then from now on I will be careful about what I buy. It is anguish having my mother, my fiancé, *and* the empress of Russia mad at me.

I feel as lonely as a bird on a roof.

After Midnight

I have just washed my face and am in my nightgown. The most comfortable place to sit at this late hour is in my bed, propped up by pillows. The candle on the tray beside my ink jug is short — only two inches tall — so I may not be able to record everything before it goes out.

To begin . . . I am exhausted after an evening of dancing. But not the sort I am used to.

I was dressed as a boy!

Everything began this afternoon when a lady-in-waiting delivered an invitation to a ball. It was written in script on fine stationery, with the odd requirement to wear men's clothing. I raised my eyebrow with curiosity.

"It's an order, miss," said the lady. "By Her Imperial Majesty."

The only place I knew to go for such a wardrobe was Peter. When I knocked on his apartment door, he opened it himself and greeted me warmly, with a kiss on each cheek. It was as if he had never been angry with me.

Peter, too, was wondering about his invitation because *he* was ordered to dress in *girls'* clothing. As we looked through his armoire we fell to giggling. I was amused to see him blush when he asked about my hoopskirt and bonnet.

By the scheduled hour we were attired in each other's outfits — I even dabbed rouge on his cheeks!

More to tell, but this candle is . . .

Next Day — About the Masquerade Ball

When the grand duke and I arrived in the ballroom we waited in the entryway, not sure which way to go. An orchestra was just beginning to play a waltz. As we stepped inside, we noticed a man striding across the room to greet us. He was tall and strikingly handsome. He wore a powdered wig, a vest, breeches buckled at the knee, and white stockings. The heels of his black shoes added a few inches to his height and made heavy steps at his approach.

"*Bonsoir,*" the man said in a feminine voice. It was the empress!

Only when I looked around did I realize the women in hoopskirts were actually men. They seemed ill at ease and their makeup did little to disguise their freshly shaved faces. The women wearing men's breeches looked equally hideous because of their bosoms and broad hips.

I, too, was prickly within my odd clothing. Dancing was hard. When the music began, I stumbled quite a bit trying to reverse my steps as if I were a boy leading a girl. I did not like it one bit, but I played along in order to please the empress.

Peter, however, did not seem to care what his aunt thought. In a fit of frustration, he tore off his skirt and, stepping out of the hoop, kicked it into a corner and stormed out of the ballroom.

I think the men wished to do the same but did not dare.

The empress seemed to relish her masculine role and the discomfort of her guests.

If she was still displeased with me on the matter of money, she gave no hint. When one of the waltzes ended, she took me to the food table, where she poured us some red wine. She lifted her glass in a toast, clinked it against mine, then, tilting her head back, drank every last drop.

I was dizzy after my drink, and even now when I'm in bed my stomach is queasy.

Mother was not invited to the ball.

13 November 1744, Moscow

The days are cold with wind and pale sunlight. Sometimes there's a scent of snow in the air, but so far the earth is still brown.

Every Tuesday, the empress hosts a masquerade ball like the last one. Unlike the costume parties of my youth, we do not get to choose our disguises. By royal order it is always the same: Men dress as women and vice versa.

To me this is vulgar entertainment. I do as I am told, but Peter refuses.

This evening while a pecan tart was being served for dessert, he whispered that he did not feel well. I pressed my hand to his cheeks. He was burning up! Right away, I called for the doctor who resides on the floor above ours.

There was much flurrying and scurrying as attendants carried him to bed and ushered me to my apartment.

We are being kept apart in case he's contagious.

Next Day

My fiancé has measles!

Because I have not yet had them, we are not allowed to be in the same room together. His illness concerns me because of a grim memory from years ago. During the first snowfall of autumn, several children in our village became sick with measles and, one by one, they perished.

What will the empress do with me if Peter dies?

Another Afternoon

I have begun to miss the company of my fiancé. It has been several days since we last spoke, but his attendants assure me he is out of danger. I hope this is the truth.

Today more than ever I miss Papá, Friedrich, and baby Ulrike. I wonder what they're doing right now and I pray my brother is well again.

19 November 1744, Moscow

This morning during breakfast an equerry brought a message saying the grand duke was no longer ill and that he wished to see his grand duchess, me.

Imagine my surprise when I entered Peter's suite. His toy soldiers were lined up in the deep windowsill, facing the gray sky. Standing at attention were his three dwarfs, their short little legs hidden by boots that were too big for them. They saluted Peter, then saluted me.

"Colonel Catherine," they said in unison.

Peter called from bed, where he sat among a mountain of feathered quilts. "You have been promoted, Figchen," he said.

I looked around the room and noticed the rat — General Fitzroy — on his leash, sniffing the floor below the breakfast tray. His red jacket had gold buttons down each side and his tail was as long as his body.

"Promoted?" I did not know what else to say.

"Come in, come in," he cried. "The game has just begun."

So that is how we spent our day, playing war with General Fitzroy and the troops.

29 November 1744, Moscow

Now that Peter's health has returned, we are packing up again. The empress wants to be in St. Petersburg in time for Christmas.

Everyone is relieved that the grand duke recovered from the measles, especially me! I was terrified wondering what would happen if he had died, though I dared not speak of my fear. Mother certainly worried aloud for the both of us, when we were alone. She was frantic, imagining the disgrace of being sent away.

Alas, dear diary, I am not looking forward to more travel, especially by sledge. It is frightfully cold out, and the wind roars as if it is in a hurry to get someplace. Oh, to stay where it is warm! The fireplace in my room is such a comfort.

St. Petersburg will be even colder because it is much farther north, on a bay that opens up to the Baltic Sea. It is always damp near the ocean, with a chill that reaches into your bones. I remember this from my homeland, for Stettin is also on a bay below the Baltic.

As I write at my desk by the window, I can see out, far

below, where snow has gathered in the courtyards and quiet streets. It has not stopped falling since early this morning. If *I* am cold sitting here with a feather quilt over my shoulders, I can only imagine how it is for the guards pacing by the gates. From this far up they look like small furry animals.

Finally, to bed . . . my *warm* bed.

18 December 1744, Tver

Dates have become a blur. The only reason I know *today's* is because it is the empress's birthday — she's thirty-five years old. Upon leaving Moscow, she had insisted on being here, in this city, for the occasion. And so here we are.

Our sledges pulled up to the palace about three o'clock this afternoon, just as the sun was setting. I was so stiff with cold, two gentlemen-in-waiting wrapped me in a fur and carried me inside. A hot bath was drawn immediately. Other ladies, including Mother, also suffered terribly from the raw weather, but they had to walk in on their own. The speed of our convoy was so brisk that at least two horses fell dead in their tracks.

Our suite overlooks the Volga River, which is white with ice. There were no children playing outside today because of the cold. A chamberlain said that with the wind, the temperature is more than thirty degrees below zero, Fahrenheit.

I must set down my pen and close these pages. Mother has been admitted into my suite and is arranging my wardrobe. She wants me to wear my blue gown with the fur collar. The party begins in an hour.

After my bath, a servant whispered to me that during dinner Mother shall be seated at a table away from mine, with other ladies of the court. I do hope she will not make a scene about this.

Before Bed

Finally, a quiet moment! The empress's party was noisy as usual, with dancing and music, card playing and roars of laughter. But Peter did not join in. He looked pale. He did not laugh or tease me in his usual manner, something that now has me worried.

Must get to bed now. Tomorrow we leave early for Shatilovo, the halfway mark to St. Petersburg.

We Are in Shatilovo Now

An alarming event!

Upon our arrival, I observed Peter getting out of his

sledge in front of ours. But after taking a few steps, he collapsed in the snow! Two soldiers rushed to his side and carried him indoors. Without even putting on my extra fur, I ran after them.

When I reached the top of the staircase, a chamberlain stopped me from entering the room where they had taken Peter.

"The grand duke has a fever, Your Highness," the man said, "and spots. We have orders to keep you at a distance in case he's contagious."

I felt low in spirit as servants showed Mother and me to our room. I'm here now, writing at a small table in front of the fireplace. A yellow cat is keeping me company, in my lap. She is purring as if we're old friends, which has cheered me up. Dinner will be in a few minutes and still I must dress.

Poor Peter. I know how miserable it is to be sick, especially so soon after his last illness. And what do the spots mean? More measles?

I forgot to mention that the empress's sledge stopped just long enough to change horses, then off she continued with her entourage. As long as the skies are clear they will travel through the long, cold night.

She has no idea that the grand duke is ill.

Next Night, Shatilobo

Oh, dear diary, bad news indeed.

This morning after breakfast I fetched Mother from her room so she and I could visit Peter. A guard standing outside his door told us to wait in the hallway. In a moment, the court physician appeared. His face was grim.

He uttered one word that stunned me. I thought my heart would stop.

"Smallpox."

My knees weakened. He caught me in his arms as I slid to the floor.

Smallpox.

A horrid disease. Like the plague, almost always fatal.

It is now after midnight, but I cannot bring myself to sleep. Mother took the news so hard she fainted and was carried off to bed, where she was given a draught of laudanum. She and I are alone in this vast, frozen country, without friends and possibly without a future.

Courtiers have been dispatched at a gallop, to catch up with the empress. She must be informed as soon as possible that her nephew might not live to see Christmas.

Eight Hours Later

When Mother recovered from her drugged sleep, she had herself announced at my room, then informed me that she and I are leaving tomorrow at dawn. Already she has ordered our sledge and horses to be ready as well as our staff. Because the empress is not here, Mother is doing as she pleases.

"Figchen, we cannot afford to be exposed." Then she reminded me that her brother died of smallpox while betrothed to Empress Elizabeth — this is how Her Imperial Majesty came to favor me over other girls when considering a bride for the grand duke. I am related to her beloved fiancé.

Alas, dear diary, once again I am getting ready for bed with a heavy heart. More travel tomorrow! The weather is bitterly cold. All afternoon the sky was gray with snow flurries and wind.

I worry Mother is pushing too hard. In my heart, I want to stay near Peter — he is my future husband! It is wrenching to think we may never again see each other. What will the empress do when she discovers Mother is disobeying orders?

Several Days Later, St. Petersburg

I've lost track of the calendar.

Many things unsettle me. Namely Peter's health, but also what the empress might think of me.

What happened is this:

While on the road, our convoy came to a sudden stop. When I pulled back the curtain to look out, I noticed the empress's sledge coming from the opposite direction, slowing to a stop. Her soldiers questioned our coachmen, then there was a snap of the reins and the royal sledge drew next to ours — but only for a moment — long enough for the empress to cast us a look of anger.

"*Vinovata, Matuska*," I mouthed to her. I am at fault, ma'am.

Then her curtain closed, and her entourage continued south. She had received word about Peter and was returning to Shatilovo to care for him.

Though the empress said nothing to us in passing, there was no mistaking her disappointment. Perhaps she feels that I have deserted my fiancé — which indeed I have! Since her own betrothed died of smallpox, she might never forgive me.

Oh, my heart is heavy.

Even though I obeyed Mother and returned with her

to St. Petersburg, she *too* is mad at me. This morning I was in the library, at a table by the window. A light snow was falling. Its whiteness against the pane made it easy to see the letter I was writing to Peter. I was trying to express myself in Russian, for I knew the empress would also read the letter.

When Mother demanded to know what I was saying, I hesitated. By habit I was thinking in French, and now needed to translate the Russian words to German so she would understand. But before I could explain, she slapped me hard across the cheek.

"Ungrateful child," she said. "How dare you hide things from your mother!"

I could not hold back my tears. Without further word, she turned to leave, the flare of her skirt leaving a cold draft.

Christmas Eve, 1744, St. Petersburg

A letter arrived today from the empress while I was sitting with my ladies over afternoon tea. I stood up and rushed to hold it near the light of a window, then broke open the seal and read her words as quickly as possible. Fortunately, she had written in French, not Russian.

I was relieved to learn my fiancé was still alive, though he is still in and out of delirium and his fever persists. The empress said she has not left Peter's room. A cot is near his bed, where she catches a nap when he's able to sleep. Despite her vanity, she doesn't seem to be worried that she, too, could catch this terrible disease and become disfigured. I admire her courage.

I expected to be scolded for not staying in Shatilovo, but instead she praised my progress with Russian. I wonder if she knows my tutor helped correct my terrible, terrible grammar!

We are in the Winter Palace, a dreary place. The halls are not decorated for Christmas, nor are there plans for a holiday banquet. It is as if it is just any other week in December: gray, cold, and without cheer.

Russia seems more bleak than my homeland.

Christmas Day, 1744, St. Petersburg

We enjoyed a small celebration after all. Mother gave our ladies gifts of pearl earrings and me a small portrait of herself, small enough to fit in my palm. It must have been painted while we still lived in Zerbst, for I've not seen any artists with easels.

"To remember me by," she said when I pulled off the ribbon and paper. I fought back tears, knowing the days with my mother will soon end.

I am in my room now, by the fire. Dear diary, I cannot seem to stop crying. If Peter dies from smallpox — as so many do — I will be sent away.

If he survives, we will marry, which means Mother will then leave Russia. Though she is disagreeable, she is still my mother and I will miss her.

The Empress's Gift to Me

Imagine my surprise when a porter came to my apartment this afternoon with a basket that appeared to have something alive inside. I lifted the lid and found an English toy spaniel staring up at me, wagging his bobbed tail.

Oh, how I love my new pet! Already my ladies are sewing him miniature outfits so we can dress him up. He is a sweet cuddly thing that has broken the winter gloom. I've named him Ivan Ivanovitch after one of the diplomats who also has black curly hair and black eyes.

1 January 1745, St. Petersburg

One year ago today I was sitting at the dinner table in Zerbst, enjoying the company of my parents, brother, and baby sister. It was snowing outside when the mysterious letter arrived.

Now I am in the window seat of a Russian palace, betrothed to my cousin, who may be dying of smallpox. Mother has made an enemy of just about everyone, and Papá is forbidden to visit me. I have a new name, a new religion, a new title. Gifts of diamonds and jewels are at my fingertips, and I may become the empress of all Russia.

How could I ever have imagined these things?

When I go to bed at night, Ivan Ivanovitch curls up on the pillow next to mine. I whisper my secrets to him, and he wags his tails as if he understands every word. He is the same size as General Fitzroy but much softer to hold.

3 January 1745, St. Petersburg

I am writing a book! Actually, it is just a pamphlet full of my thoughts and observations. The title is *Portrait of a Philosopher of Fifteen*. Perhaps I'll send it to my little sister, Ulrike, when she learns to read.

Despite the cold, I went outside this morning for fresh air, wearing the warm pelisse and tippet the empress gave me nearly a year ago. I wrapped my puppy in a fur muff and held him close to my chest so he would not freeze. Just his black nose could be seen sniffing the air. As I walked, the snow squeaked under my boots, my breath made frost. Feeling the low sunlight on my face lifted my spirits more than I thought possible, and I returned to my room with new optimism.

And a new plan.

I'm going to continue my Russian as if I will become this country's ruler, and read as many books as possible. If the grand duke dies, I want Empress Elizabeth to consider me a worthwhile companion. It will be important to converse with her about culture and politics.

Perhaps she will not send me away after all.

After an Afternoon in the Palace Library

On one of the shelves behind glass, I found two ancient texts written in French. They are Plutarch's *Lives of Great Men* and the famous speeches by Cicero. Another volume that I brought back to my desk was published in 1734, *Causes of Greatness and Decadence of the Roman Republic* by Montesquieu.

I love history! Already I'm learning how great leaders can do stupid things.

Next Day

More snow. The river is frozen solid. I am told it will be at least three months before ships are able to sail into the port of St. Petersburg. Such a long winter!

For hours every day I read in my window seat, Ivan Ivanovitch on a cushion beside me. This morning I dressed him in a blue-and-white sailor costume — the tiny cap has holes for his ears. At breakfast, I set him on the table so he could eat from a saucer. When he had finished, he walked over to Mother. Before she could shoo him away, he had dragged a sausage from her plate into the center of the table. There he remained, his front paws holding it down as he gnawed on it.

Mother turned red and covered her mouth with a napkin. I expected her to erupt, but after a moment I realized she was laughing! If my sister, brother, or I had stolen a sausage we would have been whipped. Ivan Ivanovitch does not know how spoiled he is.

I write to Peter every day.

15 January 1745, St. Petersburg

A letter arrived from the empress. Peter is recovering from smallpox and soon will be well enough to travel! They will leave Shatilovo in two weeks — I cannot wait to see him again.

This evening my ladies and I dressed Ivan Ivanovitch as a general. His crimson coat buttoned under his stomach and a pretend sword was strapped to his side. He has grown used to having a hat tied under his chin. His appearance at dinner caused much merriment among the guests — there were twenty of us. He seemed to enjoy himself because, at the sound of our laughter, he raised his head and marched upon the white tablecloth as if inspecting his officers.

20 January 1745, St. Petersburg

A courier arrived last night saying the empress plans to begin her journey tomorrow. Peter still is not robust, so they will travel just a few hours each day, stopping overnight so he will have a warm bed.

Mother is so relieved the grand duke isn't dead that she spent the morning reminding me of his good qualities. I was astounded. Now she says he is smart, well bred, and handsome.

"You have so much in common." She meant our native language (which we do not speak together), our Lutheranism (which we no longer practice), our youth (which means we have no experience with love or marriage), and our royal titles (which means people want us to favor them).

I think Mother just wants to make sure I will not change my mind when I see Peter again.

"Smallpox leaves scars," she said.

I know that.

1 February 1745, St. Petersburg

There was a scuffle in the kitchen this morning after breakfast. I had set Ivan Ivanovitch on the floor after he had eaten from his saucer. In an instant, he ran from beneath my chair, around a corner — I could hear his paws clicking and slipping along the marble hallway. Suddenly, there was a crash of pans and the shriek of female voices.

I hurried after him. The kitchen was a mess of spilled pots and overturned stools. My puppy was in the pantry — barking ferociously — where he had cornered a rat his size.

This was not a nice rat with a halter and red jacket like General Fitzroy, but a mean one. It was dirty and thin. Its lips were curled back so you could see its sharp teeth and that it was ready to attack. I grabbed Ivan's short tail and pulled him out of the pantry. As I did, the rat scurried under a shelf and disappeared.

All in all, it was the most exciting event this winter.

On a calmer note, I'm writing my "book" in French and already there are twenty pages. When I am finished, I will copy it into German so Ulrike and Friedrich will be able to read it.

Another Late Night

It is with heaviness of heart that I write this. A maid has turned down the quilt on my bed and filled a basin with warm water so I can wash my face, but I am too distressed to sleep.

The empress and grand duke returned today. At four o'clock this afternoon I was called into the grand hall. I wondered at its darkness, as there were just a few candles burning.

The sight of Peter standing in the shadows took my breath away. He was wearing a wig too big for his head, and he was wretchedly thin. But it was his face that made it difficult to draw near. I could not bring myself to embrace him.

"Hello, Figchen," he said in a hoarse voice.

I regret now that I was unable to speak and thus hurried from the room.

I have been here ever since. My dinner tray is sitting untouched at the side of my bed.

Peter is pitifully disfigured. The pockmarks covering his face are deep, the size of coins. It is weak of me to say this, but I wonder if I can go through with the marriage.

How I miss Papá. I wish he and my brother and sister were here to remind me of my carefree days from childhood.

Next Morning

The empress has excused me from banquets and official duties so Peter and I can become reacquainted, but so far we have not spoken. He refuses to be seen in public. I do not know what to do or how to apologize for rejecting him.

As I sit here at my desk, Ivan Ivanovitch is by my feet, wagging his tail and looking up at me, as if trying to cheer me. Oh, what a loyal friend is a dog who loves you.

9 February 1745, St. Petersburg

One year ago today, Mother and I arrived in this frozen city. I was full of hope for the future. Now I'm not sure of anything.

10 February 1745, St. Petersburg

The grand duke is seventeen years old today. The empress and I dined alone because he wouldn't leave his apartment. I stopped by to wish him well, but he was busy with his toy soldiers and General Fitzroy (who has a new blue jacket). Peter did not even look at me.

During dinner, the empress spoke to me in Russian, showering me with compliments that I understood quite well.

"You are pretty, my child," she said, "and getting more lovely each day." She also praised my Russian even though I speak slowly. Many of the phrases I have to first arrange in my head, then translate, *then* try to pronounce properly.

The servants and court followers have noticed the empress's attentions and now treat me in kind. You could say that people are fawning over me.

It makes me feel good, but I know her intent. Her Imperial Majesty wants me to melt under her flattery — and everyone else's — so that I shall want to stay here forever. She wants me to want Peter for a husband.

She need not worry. I have been doing a lot of thinking this past week.

Even though my fiancé is an unappealing man-child who still plays with dolls, he is my future. Without him I return to Germany, disgraced and a pauper. Without him I have no chance of wearing the Russian crown.

So marriage it is.

Our Wedding Date

Empress Elizabeth set the calendar for the twenty-first of August, six months away. By then, ice along the Neva River will have melted and ships of supplies will have been able to cross the Baltic Sea from all foreign ports.

As this will be the first royal wedding in St. Petersburg, Her Imperial Majesty wants it to be the grandest, most talked-about event ever. She has placed orders for the latest style of Parisian bonnets and hoops, as well as Naples silk and other textiles to use for dresses and wall hangings. There will be new liveries and carriages, German tableware, and Flemish linens. From the courts of Dresden and Versailles, she has requested details about ceremony and protocol from the recent weddings of August III and the dauphin. She also ordered copies to be made of Louis XV's chairs and chandeliers.

August twenty-first will be late summer, affording pleasant travel for the dignitaries and royals who are invited. Empress Elizabeth told me the guest list is already nearing one thousand.

I did not ask why my own Papá, brother, and sister are not allowed to attend.

Another Day

My ladies and I have taught Ivan Ivanovitch to walk on his hind legs. At the table, we tuck a napkin under his chin and let him eat where he pleases. He fancies *paté des foies-de-boeuf,* beef liver, with a saucer of cream. Soon he shall be plump as a priest. When we clap our hands, up he goes to dance on two legs like a little man. This evening at dinner he wore a pink silk jacket with a gentleman's hat, a downy feather in its brim.

1 March 1745, St. Petersburg

It is still cold out, but each day the sun rises higher in the sky, warming the earth bit by bit. The season of Lent is soon. I am not yet used to the Orthodox rituals, so am not sure what is expected of me.

17 March 1745, St. Petersburg

Devastating news . . . I can scarcely breathe, it has so crushed my mother and me.

This afternoon, we were alone in the sun parlor enjoying tea and scones. A chamberlain came in through the glass door, handed Mother a letter, then left. I could tell by the script that it was from Papá in Zerbst.

Mother broke open the seal in a cheerful manner, then began reading. But the expression on her face turned to shock. The letter slipped from her fingers to the floor, and she started to weep.

When I leaned down to pick it up, I read the words, " . . . *little Ulrike is dead* . . . " My throat tightened as I struggled to read the rest of the letter.

Papá wrote that it was the same illness Friedrich had, but Ulrike was so tiny and frail that she never recovered. My baby sister! She wasn't even three years old.

I don't know how to comfort Mother. For a long while we sat in the waning sunlight, not saying anything; then I remembered Ivan Ivanovitch. When I brought her my puppy she stroked his head and allowed him to lick her face. He snuggled by her neck, letting her cry into his fur.

"Thank you, Figchen," she said.

At that moment, I loved my mother more than ever.

Next Day

Mother grieves because she was unable to attend my sister's funeral. Of course by the time we received Papá's letter the sad event had already occurred. Not since my brother Wilhelm died have I seen her so devastated.

The doctor says I must drink milk and seltzer water every morning to build up my strength. The taste is more dreadful than vodka, but I will do as I am told.

Easter Has Come and Gone. . . .

Please forgive me, dear diary, but I have not been faithful about writing. The religious ceremonies of Lent, Good Friday, and Easter were shadowed by my sister's death. I went through the motions but felt little joy. It will take time, I know, to remember Ulrike without crying.

Mother and I have grown close these past weeks as we walk in the greening gardens. Spring is any day now; we can feel it in the cool air. Birds chatter in the trees overhead, ice along the river is brown from snow melting into the dirt.

There is a measure of peace between us, though I know we must part in three months. My wedding date draws near.

24 March 1745, St. Petersburg

Today the empress told me I am fluent in Russian!

I protested, citing my accent and limited vocabulary, but she said, "Nonsense, my child. If you can express yourself and comprehend what others are saying, then you are fluent. Never mind about your accent."

Now whenever she and I dine together or meet in the courtyard, we speak only Russian. It feels as though I have become her daughter, such is the affection she shows me.

Peter, on the other hand, *understands* our new language, but still responds in German. His nonchalance frustrates me. How can he and I ever become close if he does not care? It is no secret that he drinks quite a lot of wine and other spirits.

Dear diary, I do not look forward to spending my future with a stranger.

21 April 1745, St. Petersburg

My sixteenth birthday.

The empress has given me a practical gift: eight Russian maids all about my age. Her purpose is so that I will be able to practice the language night and day. She said my fluency will increase if I stop reverting back to German, which I do when Mother and I are alone together.

Two of the maids are dwarfs. They stand as tall as my rib cage and wear the dearest little shoes, as if made for dolls. Their assignment is to take care of my powder, rouge, combs, hairpins, and *mouches* — the tiny black patches ladies of the court put on their faces as beauty marks and to make their complexions look more pale. They also hide blemishes and pockmarks. Though I have a snuffbox full of these patches, I do not like to stick things on my face that look like insects — *mouche* is the French word for fly!

Duties for the other six maids are to manage my wardrobe, ribbons, linen, lace, and jewels. Also, they will look after my furniture to make sure it is polished. Together, the nine of us are cheerful and talkative. The empress does not know this yet, but we like to close the apartment doors and play tag wearing blindfolds. Ivan Ivanovitch takes to our game, barking and chasing after us as if he is the general.

I love being around young happy girls! It's also quite stimulating to hear nothing spoken but Russian. At night, the words flood my dreams.

3 May 1745

Mother and I are staying on the Fontanka River in a small stone cottage that adjoins an old house of Peter the Great. Some distance away is a summer palace where my fiancé and the empress have taken up residence. These buildings can be used only a few months of the year because there are no fireplaces for heat. Though the nights are still cool, I am warm under my quilt of goose feathers.

Already I have been measured for my wedding gown, based on instructions from the empress. Artists have presented her with ideas, then her ladies-in-waiting bring the drawings to the dressmakers who then come to my apartment. I stand still for an hour at a time while they measure, pin, and drape material about my body.

The actual fabric has yet to arrive, but the sketches show an elegant gown of silver brocade in the Spanish style, which means short sleeves and a tight waist with a full Velasquez-type skirt. Attached to the shoulders will be a cloak of silver lace studded with various jewels that the empress has given me. The seams are to be embroidered with silver roses.

I suspect my gown will be torturously heavy — and on my wedding day I must wear it for hours! At least the short sleeves will be cooler than long ones.

Peter, too, will be dressed in white, although I have not seen the drawings.

The maids told me the empress's gown would be sewn from chestnut-colored silk from Italy, also styled on Spanish lines. I do not know why Her Imperial Majesty has chosen fashion and fabrics from these faraway countries.

No one has offered to help Mother with her wardrobe. She has been ordered, however, not to wear black. Come August twenty-first, she must pretend that she no longer mourns for Ulrike.

A Warm Spring Day

The empress probably will not allow me to bring Ivan Ivanovitch to the wedding. Even so, I drew a picture in this journal of my puppy in a gentleman's outfit and tore out the page. The ladies looked at it and have promised to sew the design from leftover material. The silver jacket will look striking against his black fur and, of course, there will be a *chapeau* in the French style. I think he would look dashing with a cravat around his neck.

18 May 1745, Peterhof

Dear diary, I am sorry that another fortnight has passed without writing. We have moved again! This palace was built by Peter the Great and is on the coast, almost twenty miles south of St. Petersburg. We are on the Gulf of Finland with a sweeping view of the ocean. Small fishing boats look like toys upon the water. Now and then a yacht sails by on its way to port.

The empress is far away, visiting one of her monasteries. I am thankful she did not force us to travel with her. She said this is a good time for Peter and me to rest, because after our wedding much will be expected of us.

I love it here. We dine outside under a canopy, the air free from gnats and mosquitoes because of the sea breeze. I am lulled by the waves breaking upon the shore and the *clickity-clack* as they wash over the pebbly beach, back into the surf.

The grand duke and I, or Mother and I — never the three of us together — take long walks along the dunes. I am enjoying the lengthening days. Soon I hope to see the northern lights paint the sky. When they do appear, I will try to coax my fiancé outside so we can watch the colors together.

Later

I am sitting on a blanket in the warm sand. The wind keeps blowing off my sun hat, so I have tied its ribbon under my chin. Seagulls are circling overhead as Peter tosses bread crusts in the air. To me, the gulls' cries are a lovely, free sound.

Oh . . . Peter is calling me to put away my pen and ink. He has noticed the tide is low and there are pools to explore. Will close these pages for now, dear diary.

I'm going with him.

Epilogue

On August 21, 1745, at three o'clock in the afternoon, a procession of one hundred and twenty carriages escorted Catherine and Peter to the cathedral of Kazan. Their own carriage was drawn by eight white horses and was surrounded by dignitaries on horseback marching at a snail's pace. Crowds of observers along the streets of St. Petersburg fell to their knees as the elegant teenage couple passed by. The religious ceremony lasted several hours and the festivities continued for ten days.

One month later, Catherine's mother left Russia. The Princess of Anhalt-Zerbst wanted to spare her daughter an emotional scene, so she rose before dawn and departed without saying good-bye. When Catherine discovered her mother's empty apartment she burst into tears. Now she felt more alone than ever.

Life in the Russian court became like a prison to

Catherine. Not only was her marriage a disaster, her every move was watched and criticized. She was no longer allowed to play games with her maids, and people with whom she formed close relationships were soon deported or reassigned. Empress Elizabeth forbade her to write to her parents without first being censored by the College of Foreign Affairs, forcing her to copy "form letters," word for word.

Years later, Catherine wrote of these experiences in her memoirs: "In short, a thousand horrors of which I have forgotten half . . . I had led a life which would have rendered ten other women mad and twenty others in my place would have died of a broken heart."

Catherine had three children: Paul Petrovich, Anna Petrovna (who died in infancy), and Alexis Bobrinski. In 1762, seventeen years after her wedding, Catherine was proclaimed empress and reigned for thirty-four years. Upon her death at the age of sixty-six, her son Paul ascended the throne.

Life in Russia
in 1744

Historical Note

On Christmas Day, 1761, Empress Elizabeth died and the reign of Catherine's husband, Peter III, began. It was short-lived. One of Peter's first acts as emperor was to sign a peace treaty with King Frederick II of Prussia, ending Russia's role in the Seven Years War. All conquered lands were returned to Prussia. Peter's deep admiration for that country outraged leaders of the Russian army, which had suffered great losses in the war.

Meanwhile, Catherine feared for her life. She was afraid Peter would install his mistress as his wife and banish or kill her. Accordingly, in June 1762, Catherine achieved a bloodless coup with the aid of military and religious leaders. Peter refused to fight for his crown and died in custody six days later, supposedly after an argument with his guards. Thus began the long reign of Catherine II.

Many thought her time on the throne would also be short-lived. She had no Russian blood. She was born in the

Prussian province of Pomerania, the daughter of a minor German princess and an Army officer. But Catherine proved her critics wrong and ruled for thirty-four years as sole autocrat of all Russia.

The new empress immediately set about restoring order and prosperity to a country drained by war and royal neglect. Charges of corruption and injustice were everywhere. The country was bankrupt. It is said she worked relentlessly from early morning to late night on affairs of state.

She first encouraged agricultural reform, realizing that Russia's future was in its land and resources. New crops and techniques were implemented, modern machinery was imported from England, and foreign workers were recruited to resettle in Russia. Catherine then ordered a full survey of the country's mineral resources and established Russia's first School of Mining to train geologists and workers.

She also promoted the establishment of new factories, particularly for linens and leather goods. By abolishing export duties, she revitalized Russia's foreign trade, so much so that in about five years, the country was no longer bankrupt. The number of factories while she was on the throne increased from 984 to more than 3,000.

In 1781, the construction of the Siberian highway was begun.

Later in her reign, Catherine turned her skills to health care, education, and the arts. She promoted a vaccination for smallpox, the biggest killer of children, and was the first inoculated, to demonstrate that the vaccine worked. She decreed that every province would have a hospital and founded a College of Medicine to train doctors.

Likewise, she implemented a plan so that every town would have a school staffed with teachers, and founded a boarding school for girls. One of her crowning achievements was the construction of the Hermitage in St. Petersburg, which houses the art she avidly collected. It remains one of the world's greatest art museums. And her appreciation for literature inspired her to purchase Voltaire's books after his death and those of the encyclopedist Denis Diderot. During her reign, the imperial library grew from a few hundred books to thirty-eight thousand. She also initiated the *Imperial Russian Dictionary*, which included vocabulary from two hundred languages.

In 1766, she granted freedom of worship in Russia.

During her lifetime, Catherine was offered the title of "The Great" but declined. "I leave it to posterity to judge impartially what I have done," she said.

Catherine never remarried. Her son Paul succeeded her when she died of a stroke in 1796.

Some interesting world events during the reign of Catherine the Great:

∾ The metric system was developed in France, as was the first hot-air balloon.

∾ During the French Revolution, a "humane" instrument for beheading criminals was developed by physician J. I. Guillotin. This first "guillotine" to be erected in the Place de Revolution, Paris, was used for the execution of King Louis XVI and Queen Marie Antoinette in 1793.

∾ The English astronomer Sir William Herschel discovered the planet Uranus.

∾ Beethoven's first compositions were published.

∾ London introduced a system for numbering houses and laid its first paved sidewalk.

∾ The potato became the most popular food in Europe.

༄ Mutineers of H.M.S. *Bounty* settled on the Pitcairn Islands in the eastern Pacific Ocean.

༄ The slave trade was abolished in the French colonies and Denmark; an English settlement was founded in Sierra Leone for freed slaves.

༄ James Cook sailed around the world, the first European to explore Hawaii.

༄ The American Revolution resulted in the thirteen colonies declaring their independence from England.

༄ George Washington delivered his farewell address after refusing to accept a third term as president of the United States. This was in 1796, the year of Catherine's death.

Duchy of Schleswig-Holstein-Gottorp
(Denmark, Norway, Sweden)

The Romanov Dynasty

♛ **Frederick III** $\overset{m.}{=}$ **Maria Elizabeth**
King of Denmark and Norway

♛ **Peter I** $\overset{m.}{=}$ ♛ **Catherine I**
(The Great)

♛ **Christian V** $\overset{m.}{=}$ **Frederica Amalia**

Albertina $\overset{m.}{=}$ **Christian Augustus** ♛ **Frederick IV** $\overset{m.}{=}$ **Hedwig Sophia**
of Sweden

Anna Petrovna   ♛ **Elizabeth I**

Christian $\overset{m.}{=}$ **Johanna Elizabeth**
of Anhalt-Zerbst

Charles Frederick $\overset{m.}{=}$ ♛ **Peter III**

Friedrich   Elizabeth   ♛ **Catherine II**

♛ **Paul I** $\overset{m.}{=}$ **Sophia Dorothea**
of Wurttenberg

Louise $\overset{m.}{=}$ ♛ **Alexander I**   Constantine   Helen   Maria   Catherine   Anna   ♛ **Nicholas I** $\overset{m.}{=}$ **Charlotte**
of Baden   *of Prussia*

☐ **♛ = Ruler**

Catherine the Great, Family Tree

Catherine the Great: Born in Stettin, Pomerania, on April 21, 1729, as Princess Sophie Augusta Fredericka of Anhalt-Zerbst. Her nickname "Figchen" is from a diminutive of Sophie, *Sophiechen*, or *'fiechen*. As a child she was a boisterous tomboy, recognized even by her playmates as a natural leader. In her early teens, she was ambitious enough to envision herself as a queen or empress and do whatever necessary to achieve this powerful role. Thus, when she learned that her betrothed, Peter, was repulsive and weak, she shrugged off her disappointment. After all, it was the throne that interested her, not the marriage. It is said that after her wedding Catherine had many lovers and that her children were illegitimate, including her eldest son, who became Czar Paul I upon her death in 1796. She had ruled for thirty-four years.

Princess Johanna Elizabeth of Holstein-Gottorp: (1712-1760) Mother of Catherine. Emotionally cold and physically abusive, she was a social climber who loved court intrigues and wanted nothing more than to become famous through Figchen's marriage into Russian royalty. Her pushy, arrogant behavior infuriated Empress Elizabeth, who eventually banned her from regular contact with Figchen and forced her to leave Russia after the wedding.

Prince Christian August Furst of Anhalt-Zerbst: (1690-1747) A major general in the Prussian army, and a Lutheran, he pleaded with Figchen not to convert to the Greek Orthodoxy of the Russian church. The last time he saw his daughter was when her sleigh left Berlin for Russia.

Mademoiselle Babette [Babet] Cardel: Figchen's beloved tutor was from a Huguenot family that had fled from France to Germany after the Edict of Nantes was revoked. She did not accompany Figchen to Russia.

Elizabeth Petrovna: (1709-1761) Czarina [Empress] of Russia. The daughter of Peter I, she ruled Russia for twenty years, never marrying. Intelligent and vivacious, she strived to make the court a center of fashion, also establishing the University of Moscow and the Academy of Arts at St. Petersburg. She died on Christmas Day, 1761, at which time her nephew the Grand Duke became Czar Peter III.

Peter: (1728-1762) Grandson of Peter the Great, he was sickly and mentally dull. He and Catherine (Figchen) were wed on August 21, 1745, but their marriage was an unhappy one. Seven months after he ascended the throne as Czar Peter III, he was assassinated. Some historians speculate that Catherine orchestrated his murder.

Catherine's brothers and sisters

- Prince Wilhelm Christian Friedrich of Anhalt-Zerbst-Dornburg (1730-1742)
- Prince Friedrich Augustus of Anhalt-Zerbst-Dornburg (1734-1793)
- Princess Auguste Christine Charlotte of Anhalt-Zerbst-Dornburg (b/d 1736—lived two weeks)
- Princess Elizabeth Ulrike (1742-1745). This sister died at age 2½ when her mother was in Russia with Figchen; her godmother was Empress Elizabeth.

Portrait of Catherine II, painted in 1745.

Portrait of Peter Ulrich, who became Catherine's husband and Czar Peter III.

A royal portrait of Catherine II, Peter III, and their son Paul.

A spray of diamonds from the Russian crown jewels owned by Catherine II.

A painting of Catherine riding horseback sits above Peter the Great's royal throne in one of Peter the Great's palaces near St. Petersburg.

A letter, handwritten in French, from Johanna Elizabeth to Empress Elizabeth I of Russia.

Portrait of Catherine's mother, Johanna Elizabeth, Princess of Anhalt-Zerbst.

Portrait of Elizabeth I, Empress of Russia.

An engraving showing Elizabeth's summer palace in St. Petersburg.

A view of Moscow and the Kremlin.

A map showing Prussia and Russia in 1744.

Author's Note

I would like to thank Elaine Kraft, Librarian for the Pommerscher Verein Freistadt in Mequon, Wisconsin, for her generous and enthusiastic assistance with photos, maps, recipes, and other research material related to Catherine's childhood in Pomerania.

The most interesting source for this Royal Diary was Catherine herself. She left behind personal letters, diplomatic papers, and several autobiographical accounts, most of which were written in French. These memoirs are a fascinating glimpse into her vigorous personality and court intrigues, but because she wrote them during different stages of her adult life — often retelling the same events in different detail — some accounts are confusing and contradictory. For example, in one edition she says her dog Ivan Ivanovitch was a poodle, in another she says he was a spaniel. Spellings of names and places often differ, but this might merely be from the trickiness of translation.

A few years before Catherine became empress, she threw a stack of her writings into the fire, including *Portrait of a Philosopher of Fifteen*. Now, *that* would have been interesting to read!

An estimated value of the gold ruble during Catherine's time was approximately $15 U.S. (according to Henri Troyat's 1977 biography). This means the betrothal ring she gave Peter at 14,000 rubles was probably worth about $121,000.

Kristiana Gregory is the author of several Dear America, Royal Diary, and My America titles, as well as Scholastic's Prairie River series. She lives in Boise, Idaho, with her family.

For Kip,

wonderful husband
and tender father
to our sons

Acknowledgments

Grateful acknowledgment is made for permission to reprint the following:

Cover painting by Tim O'Brien

Page 157: Portrait of Catherine the Great, bpk, Berlin.

Page 158: Portrait of Peter III, akg-images, London.

Page 159: Portrait of Catherine, Peter, and Paul, The Granger Collection, New York.

Page 160, top: Spray of diamonds, S.J. Phillips, London, UK/www.bridgeman.co.uk.

Page 160, bottom: Painting of Catherine II over throne, Steve Raymer/Corbis, New York.

Page 161, top: Johanna Elizabeth's letter, akg-images, London.

Page 161, bottom: Portrait of Johanna Elizabeth, akg-images, London.

Page 162: Portrait of Elizabeth Petrovna, Mary Evans Picture Library, London.

Page 163, top: Palace in St. Petersburg, Stapleton Collection, UK/www.bridgeman.co.uk.

Page 163, bottom: View of Moscow, akg-images, London.

Page 164: Map by Jim McMahon.

Other books in The Royal Diaries Series

ELIZABETH I
Red Rose of the House of Tudor
by Kathryn Lasky

CLEOPATRA VII
Daughter of the Nile
by Kristiana Gregory

MARIE ANTOINETTE
Princess of Versailles
by Kathryn Lasky

ISABEL
Jewel of Castilla
by Carolyn Meyer

ANASTASIA
The Last Grand Duchess
by Carolyn Meyer

NZINGHA
Warrior Queen of Matamba
by Patricia C. McKissack

KAIULANI
The People's Princess
by Ellen Emerson White

Copyright © 2005 by Kristiana Gregory

§⊙§

All rights reserved. Published by Scholastic Inc.
557 Broadway, New York, NY 10012.
SCHOLASTIC, THE ROYAL DIARIES, and associated logos are trademarks and/or
registered trademarks of Scholastic Inc.

Library of Congress Cataloging-in-Publication Data

Gregory, Kristiana.
Catherine : the great journey / by Kristiana Gregory.
p.   cm. — (The Royal Diaries)
Summary: The diary of Princess Sophie, later named Catherine, from 1743 until
1745, when at age fifteen she is married to her second cousin Peter, Grand Duke of
Russia, who will one day be Emperor. Includes historical notes on her later life.
ISBN 0-439-25385-3
[1. Catherine II, Empress of Russia, 1729–1796 — Juvenile fiction.   2. Elizabeth,
Empress of Russia, 1709–1762 — Juvenile fiction.   3. Peter III, Emperor of Russia,
1723–1762 — Juvenile fiction.   4. Catherine II, Empress of Russia, 1729–1796 —
Fiction.   5. Elizabeth, Empress of Russia, 1709–1762 — Fiction.   6. Peter III,
Emperor of Russia, 1723–1762 — Fiction.   7. Kings, queens, rulers, etc. — Fiction.
8. Diaries — Fiction.   9. Russia — History — Elizabeth, 1741–1762 — Juvenile
fiction.   10. Russia — History — Elizabeth, 1741–1762 — Fiction.]
I. Title. II. Series.
PZ7.G8619 Ca 2005
[Fic] 22   2005002373
ISBN (Paper Over Board) 0-439-25385-3

10 9 8 7 6 5 4 3   06 07 08 09

The display type was set in Galahad.
The text type was set in Augereau.
Book design by Elizabeth B. Parisi
Photo research by Amla Sanghvi

Printed in the U.S.A.   23
First edition, December 2005

§⊙§